BRUCE WEBER'S
★ INSIDE ★
BASEBALL
‹1992›

SCHOLASTIC INC.
New York Toronto London Auckland Sydney

PHOTO CREDITS

Cover: Photo of Cecil Fielder, © Jeff Carlick/Sportschrome East/West. **iv, 7, 28, 46:** Texas Rangers. **4, 12, 56:** Seattle Mariners. **6, 32:** Detroit Tigers. **8, 14, 30, 66 (left):** Boston Red Sox. **9, 36:** Baltimore Orioles. **10, 48, 66 (right):** Oakland Athletics. **11, 34:** Toronto Blue Jays. **13, 15, 52:** Minnesota Twins. **16, 20, 26, 74:** Atlanta Braves. **18, 58, 80:** San Francisco Giants. **19, 23, 62:** Chicago Cubs. **21, 72:** Cincinnati Reds. **22, 24, 27, 64:** Pittsburgh Pirates. **25, 78:** San Diego Padres. **38:** Milwaukee Brewers. **40:** New York Yankees. **42:** Cleveland Indians. **44:** Chicago White Sox. **50:** California Angels. **54:** Kansas City Royals. **60, 84:** New York Mets. **68:** Philadelphia Phillies. **70:** Montreal Expos. **76:** Los Angeles Dodgers. **82:** Houston Astros.

ISBN 0-590-45627-X

12 11 10 9 8 7 6 5 4 3 2 1   2 3 4 5 6 7/9

Printed in the U.S.A.   01

First Scholastic printing, April 1992

CONTENTS

Like Ol' Man River, O'l Man Nolan Ryan keeps rolling along. Is there another no-hitter in the strikeout king's arm?

INTRODUCTION:
Arms — and the Men

As long as men (and boys and girls) have played baseball, it has been a pitcher's game. When sports experts talk about the value of pitching, it sounds like a math exercise: "Baseball is 90% pitching!" "Baseball is 80% pitching!"

Think about last year. The Atlanta Braves, long the National League doormats, went from worst to first when John Smoltz, Tom Glavine, and Steve Avery all learned how to pitch. The Minnesota Twins, floundering since their '87 world title and last-place finish in 1990, became the 1991 champions because Jack Morris remembered how he used to blow away the AL 10 years ago and youngsters like Kevin Tapani, Scott Erickson, and Rick Aguilera all grew up.

The formula works in reverse, too. From 1984 through 1990, the New York Mets finished no lower than second in the NL East. But in 1991, Doc Gooden and Sid Fernandez got hurt, and Frank Viola forgot how to win. Result: a fifth-place flop.

Same thing in Oakland. For three years, when Bob Welch, Dave Stewart, and the rest of the A's mound gang were practically unhittable, the team was untouchable. But in '91, when most of the Athletics staff had career years (on the down side), the ball club sank to fourth, just three games out of the AL West cellar.

Bottom line: Great pitching still defeats great hitting, and consistent pitching creates consistently successful ball clubs. That doesn't mean that teams with good pitching will automatically win; it takes a lot more than that. But it does mean that teams *without* good pitching probably won't win.

As a result, teams take chances when it comes to pitching. When the Cubs' Rick Sutcliffe was available last winter, lots of folks made outrageous bids for his services. Maybe, just maybe, they reasoned, he'll return to his old form. Same thing with the Mets' Frank Viola. The one-time Cy Young award winner had gone through two so-so seasons and couldn't get anyone out the second half of '91. But Frank is a left-hander (especially valuable) who has won in the past. So clubs were talking about three-, four-, and five-year contracts for big, big bucks in the hope that this Viola can still make some sweet music.

So what does all of this mean for the 1992 season? First, the Atlanta Braves, with one of the game's finest young pitching staffs, are more likely to return to postseason play than the world champion Minnesota Twins, whose pitching isn't quite as strong — or young. Of course, the Braves' path isn't overly smooth. The L.A. Dodgers' pitching might be good enough to win, and Cincinnati has substantially upgraded its pitching (Greg Swindell and Tim Belcher). Neither San Diego nor San Francisco seems to have the arms to win the West. And believe it or not, the Astros, with fine young throwers, might be right in the hunt by 1994 or so.

Though the Pirates seem to be falling apart, the pitching remains solid, and that might be good enough for an NL East three-peat. Pitching injuries continue to hamper the Cardinals, and the Cubs and Phillies don't seem to have enough. The Mets, long the game's pitching leaders, open the '92 season with a few answers (Bret Saberhagen) and a few questions on the mound. Montreal, with so many problems, may have to deal pitching for offense.

In the AL East, nobody has a dominant staff, though Toronto remains in a position to win again, and the Yankees and Indians, like Houston, are building their mound crews with youth. The Orioles wait for Ben McDonald, the Tigers need help, and Boston always seems one arm away.

Pitching also makes the difference in the West. Minnesota probably won't win again, and pitching-rich Kansas City and California will bounce off the bottom. Offensive-minded Texas is still a pitcher or two away. Seattle should hit a lot of homers in the Kingdome, but the bullpen is suspect. If the White Sox get consistent performance from their rotation, they could win it all, unless all of the Athletics pitchers rebound from career-low seasons.

It should be fun!

— Bruce Weber
December 1991

3

Even in a domed stadium, the sky is the limit
for the Mariners' Ken Griffey, Jr., easily
baseball's finest young outfielder.

American League
ALL-PRO TEAM

First Base
CECIL
FIELDER
DETROIT TIGERS

In Detroit, where Japanese imports are frowned upon, there's one package from Tokyo that everybody loves. Cecil Fielder, who felt unloved in Toronto and spent a year finding himself in Japan, is threatening to blow away every home-run record in Detroit, even after his late start.

The wide-bodied Fielder — some Detroit Lions football players may be jealous of his size — paired his 51-homer 1990 season with a 44-homer performance in '91. That tied Oakland's Jose Canseco for the major-league home-run title. But no one came close to Fielder in the RBI department. His 133 were 11 better than anyone in the game.

Bottom line: Thanks to Fielder, Detroit stayed in the AL East hunt until the last couple of weeks of the season. That surprised everyone in the league except, perhaps, Detroit manager Sparky Anderson. "Did you hear about the one he hit in Milwaukee in September?" asked Anderson, with awe. That 502-foot blast out of County Stadium made everyone sit up and take notice.

"I've got to become an even better hitter," says Fielder. "If I hit better, I'll hit better with power. That's my goal for '92." That and an AL East title.

Second Base
JULIO FRANCO
TEXAS RANGERS

Everyone knew Julio Franco could hit. But no one ever dreamed he could hit as well as he did in 1991. Though Roberto Alomar of the Blue Jays may press him in the future, Franco figures to remain one of the top AL second sackers for years to come.

The Rangers sent three players to Cleveland for Franco after the '88 season. It ranks among the all-time deal steals. Julio's major-league-leading .341 average marked his fifth .300-plus season in the last six years. Though he had hit .319 in '87, his '91 performance finally made Franco a household name throughout the baseball world.

Another of the unending talent pool from San Pedro de Macoris in the Dominican Republic, Franco tattooed the ball at a .376 pace in August and then .367 in September and October to sew up the bat title. His first 200-hit year (201) included a league-leading 156 singles. Julio hit .348 in late-inning pressure situations and batted .332 against right-handed pitching, the league's best mark by a right-handed hitter. He also smacked a career-high 15 homers, scored 108 runs, and banged in 78 runs.

The Rangers may still be a pitcher or two away from challenging for an AL West title, but they're well set at second base.

Third Base
WADE BOGGS
BOSTON RED SOX

Some Red Sox fans are worried. They look at the team's roster and notice that Wade Boggs will turn 34 in June. Normally that would be cause for concern. Not with Boggs. This guy swats the baseball so well that he might not hit a slump until an old-timers game sometime in 2025.

He may not be scoring as many runs as he did or drawing as many walks (only 89 last year after 105 or more in four of the previous five seasons), but there's nothing he can't do with a bat in his hands. His .332 bat mark (up from a career-low .302 in '90) included 181 hits, 42 of them doubles. Only Texas's Julio Franco (.341) outhit the 6–2, 197-pound Boggs, who also finished third in the AL in on-base average (.421).

Boggs's 1991 numbers give him a 10-year career average of .345, which ranks him sixth in the *history* of the game for players with a decade or more of service. Here even Boston's beloved Ted Williams falls into line behind Boggsy. But best of all, his glove, long the subject of Wade's critics, has become an asset.

By the time Boggs decides to hang up his spikes (and turf shoes), he should be considered among the greatest who have ever played.

CAL RIPKEN
BALTIMORE ORIOLES

The hair is now flecked with gray. The once-lanky body is a little chunkier. But when Oriole Park (at Camden Yards, of course) opens this spring, Cal Ripken, Jr., will be at shortstop, thrilling Bird fans just as he has for a decade.

When Rip got off to a horrid start in 1990, baseball folks instantly pointed to "the streak" as the cause. Ripken, son of long-time Oriole coach and manager Cal Sr. and brother of second-sacker Bill, hasn't missed a start in 10 years and now stands just 3½ seasons short of Lou Gehrig's "unreachable" mark of 2,130 straight games. However, whenever Cal goes 0-for-8, the fans figure he needs a rest.

But bouncing back from a so-so .250 bat mark in '90, Ripken smacked the ball at a .323 clip (sixth in the AL) with a .566 slugging percentage (second), 34 homers (third), and 114 RBIs (fourth). Of his 210 hits (second), 85 went for extra bases — to lead the league. In September, when tired players seem to fade, Ripken was better than ever.

Even his glove work was spectacular and earned him a Gold Glove.

For all these reasons, Rip was voted the AL's MVP (sorry, Cecil Fielder), as well as our surefire AL All-Pro shortstop.

9

Outfield
JOSE CANSECO
OAKLAND ATHLETICS

If there's any current threat to Hank Aaron and Babe Ruth's all-time home-run records, it has to be Oakland strongman Jose Canseco. Unlike his current home-run rival, popular Cecil Fielder, a lot of folks don't particularly like Canseco. He usually gets booed on the road and, from time to time, even at home. His defense will never make him a candidate for a Gold Glove award. But for long-term power numbers, he's the next best hope for career home-run marks.

When Jose smacked his 200th career round-tripper last August, he boldly announced that his target was 600 to 700 homers. "If I stay healthy," he said, "I can average 35 a year. And that makes it possible."

Canseco and Fielder battled nose-to-nose for the AL homer title Fielder had won with 51 in 1990. When the dust cleared, each had smacked 44, and the overall hitting competition between the two arch-rivals was incredible. Jose wound up hitting .266 (five points better than Cecil) but trailed the Tiger in RBIs, 133–122. Canseco, however, was great in the clutch, ranking among the league leaders in hitting with runners on base, and in scoring position and two outs. That's what All-Stars do.

Outfield
JOE CARTER
TORONTO BLUE JAYS

For Joe Carter, the frustration continues. Buried for years at the bottom of the league standings with Cleveland and, for one year, San Diego, the powerful 6–3, 215-pound Carter dreamed of postseason play.

It didn't take long. Given a chance in Toronto in that memorable four-man Blue Jay-Padre trade last winter, Joe jumped on it. He hit .273, his best since 1986, with 33 homers and a personal-best 42 doubles, both ranking fourth in the AL. He also banged in 108 runs. And when Toronto began to slump late in the season, it was Oklahoma-native Carter who rallied them over the Red Sox in the final weeks.

Still, the season ended on a down note for Carter. An ankle injury in game 3 of the ALCS, suffered while tracking down a Shane Mack line drive, crippled him. Joe gave it his best shot but went 1-for-9 the rest of the way, stranding seven Toronto runners in the process.

"I've wanted to win in October so long I can taste it. That wasn't the way it was supposed to end," says Carter. "We'll be back — and I'll be back."

Anyone who has watched Carter through nine outstanding big-league seasons knows he's going to make it happen.

11

KEN GRIFFEY, Jr.
SEATTLE MARINERS

How good is Ken Griffey, Jr.? Based on his '91 performance, the official major-league ratings, and eyewitness reports out of the Kingdome, he may well be the best outfielder in the American League. How good can Ken Griffey, Jr., become? About as good as the son of the now-retired Ken Griffey, Sr., wants to be.

When the votes for the 1991 AL All-Star team were counted, the one-time Cincinnati high school superstar had won the fans' support for a starting berth. No big deal? Yes, it is, when you play in a market as small as Seattle.

But the fans knew what they were doing, even if young Ken saved his best for after the All-Star break. After lounging in the .280s for most of the first part of the season, Griffey hit over .400 for the first three weeks after the break, got his average over .300 in early August, then kept sprinting to the wire. He wound up with a sparkling .327 bat mark, a .527 slugging percentage, 65 extra-base hits (including 42 doubles), and 100 RBIs, each figure among the AL's best. There's no questioning Griffey's speed or defense, either, provided he stays on top of himself and on top of his game. If he does, the sky (even in a dome) is the limit!

Catcher
BRIAN HARPER
MINNESOTA TWINS

The book on Brian Harper is simple: good hit, questionable field. But if there were any questions about Harper's defense, the 31-year-old Minnesota backstop answered them during the Twins' spectacular World Series victory over the Atlanta Braves. The National League champs quickly learned that the Minnesota catcher was nobody to mess with in close plays at the plate. His crushing collision with Lonnie Smith will make Series highlight films forever.

The power-packed 6–2, 205-pound Harper is the AL's best-hitting catcher. No doubt about it. He could always hit. But in stints as a utility player with the Angels, Pirates, Tigers, and Athletics (he was ready to retire four years ago), the one-time fourth-round draft pick couldn't find a comfortable position. When the Twins stuck him behind the plate, he certainly found a home. "People question Brian's defense," says Minny manager Tom Kelly. "But we're totally confident in his ability back there. And you've gotta love his bat."

Brian's .311 average (plus .381 in the World Series), along with 10 homers and 69 RBIs, made him a key to the team's bounce-back from worst to first in '91. With better defense, he'll become even more valuable.

Pitcher
ROGER CLEMENS
BOSTON RED SOX

Just when you think that Roger Clemens's temper has gotten the best of him, the Red Sox's fiery right-hander comes up with one more spectacular season that certifies him as the AL's best.

A one-time U. of Texas superstar, Clemens sat out a five-game suspension last season following a nationally televised outburst against AL umpires in the 1990 play-offs. Still, the chunky Clemens managed to start 35 games for the Sox in '91 and finished 13 of them. His 10 strikeouts on the final day of the season tied the Mets' David Cone for the major-league lead in strikeouts with 241. (Cone needed 19 Ks that day to force the tie!) Meanwhile, Roger also wound up with 18 wins (10 of them away from friendly Fenway Park) and a league-leading 2.62 earned run average.

That performance got Clemens his third Cy Young award. The 6–4, 220-pounder won the coveted trophy back-to-back in 1986 and '87. Roger's 1,665 career strikeouts, while far from Nolan Ryan's all-time mark, represent an all-time Red Sox high. The previous record-holder: old Cy Young himself.

What makes the Rocket man doubly valuable to the Sox is his contract. He's signed through 1995, with an option for '96.

14

SCOTT ERICKSON
MINNESOTA TWINS

If you don't think the mere sight of Scott Erickson frightens American League hitters, then you probably haven't tried to hit against him. The black socks, black glove, and iron stare all play second string to the first-rate slider, fastball, and forkball.

"I don't even like to play catch with him," says teammate and World Series hero Jack Morris. "When you catch the ball, you need to check all your fingers."

When the 6–4, 225-pound fireballer arrived in Minnesota in 1990, the Twins were in the midst of a last-place season. His 8–4 record was hardly noticed.

But when the Twins got off to a rolling start in '91, everyone saw that Erickson was the guy getting it done. From April 21 through June 24 last season, Scott was practically unhittable and certainly unbeatable. He won 12 straight decisions, the top win streak in the majors since Roger Clemens won 14 in a row in 1986. By the All-Star break he was 12–3 with a 1.83 ERA as the Twins proved they were for real.

Arm and elbow problems limited Erickson through the final months of the season. Still he wound up 20–8 with a 3.18 earned run mark, clearly the key to the Twins' AL pennant. More should follow.

All it took was a Cy Young season from Tom Glavine, and his Atlanta Braves went from last to first in the National League.

National
League
ALL-PRO TEAM

First Base
WILL
CLARK
SAN FRANCISCO GIANTS

This is one of those too-close-to-call calls you have to make even though you'd really love to pass. San Diego's Freddy McGriff, part of that winter of '90 blockbuster trade between the Padres and Blue Jays, showed the NL that he is the real thing in his league debut. But we'll still cast our 1B vote for longtime leader Will Clark of the Giants.

Will the Thrill remains one of the few players those of us who get free tickets would pay to watch. His swing is one of the prettiest in the game, and he rarely makes a mistake at the plate. His .301 average in '91 kept his career mark at a brilliant .302. More important, his 116 RBIs set a career high, though he lost the league title to the Mets' Howard Johnson on the final day of the season. When the Giants knocked the Dodgers out of the NL race on the final Saturday of the '91 campaign, Clark tripled and scored the first run in a 4–0 San Fran victory. But his best day of the year came at the Vet in Philadelphia on July 14 when his five hits produced seven RBIs for the Giants.

Clark is equally talented in the field. His 63 consecutive errorless games helped him to a league-leading .997 fielding mark that, after all, makes the six-year veteran the best in his business.

Second Base
RYNE SANDBERG
CHICAGO CUBS

The '91 Chicago Cubs' season was nothing to write home about. By the time the bats and balls had been stored away, the Cubs were without a manager — again! — and even without a club president. But there was no hole at second base, where Ryno Sandberg is quickly carving out a Hall-of-Fame career at Wrigley Field.

A typical Sandberg year includes batting in the .300 area, 100 RBIs, 100 runs scored, and near-flawless fielding. So 1991 was typical, but only for a Sandberg. Ryne played his 100-RBI year a little close. Number 100 came on a double in his last at-bat. But it was his second straight year at that level, something no other second sacker had done in 42 years! His 104 runs scored made it three years in a row over 100.

At age 32, when lots of infielders are beginning to turn the corner toward retirement, the one-time Phillie prospect seems to be better than ever. His ninth straight Gold Glove award was won on the strength of an incredible four-error (and .995 fielding average) season, including a run of 40 straight errorless games.

A couple of NL second basemen appear headed for spectacular careers. But All-Pro? They'll just have to wait.

Third Base
TERRY
PENDLETON
ATLANTA BRAVES

If Terry Pendleton ever loses it as a ball-player, he may well have a career as a fortune-teller. As his new team, the Atlanta Braves, broke spring training a year ago, Pendleton boldly predicted: "We could win this thing. It's no sure thing, but we've got a good shot."

Go from last to first, Terry? You bet. And at the center of it all was the free-agent third baseman himself. A .230 hitter for the Cardinals in 1990, Pendleton skipped town when it seemed sure he would lose his 3B job to ex-catcher Todd Zeile.

In Atlanta, chunky Terry merely raised his batting average 89 points (to a league-leading .319), tied for the league lead in total bases (303), and topped the NL with 187 hits. He even excelled in the power department where his 22 homers marked a career best. During the final week of the '91 season, when the battle for the NL West pennant was on the line every day, Terry hit .400 (10-for-25) with two homers and seven RBIs. To top it off, he was named the NL's MVP.

"What a great feeling," says the veteran Pendleton. "I left St. Louis really down, showed up in Atlanta, and seemed to be born again. It was wonderful."

Shortstop
BARRY LARKIN
CINCINNATI REDS

The best athlete in the National League? Could well be the Reds' super shortstop, Barry Larkin. A hometown boy made good, the rangy 6–0, 185-pound Larkin does it all — hits, hits with power, runs, fields, and throws — and does it all beautifully.

For Larkin, who grew up watching the previous Red Machine (including Johnny Bench, Pete Rose, Joe Morgan, Tony Perez, and Davey Concepcion), success in his hometown is especially sweet. "Sweeping the Oakland A's to win the 1990 World Series right in my own backyard is the all-time highlight," says Larkin. "It doesn't get any better than that."

The standout in one of Cincy's premier athletic families — his brothers excel in football and basketball, Barry missed half of the 1989 season because of an elbow injury suffered in an All-Star Game contest in Anaheim, California. At the time, there were serious doubts about the rest of his career.

Forget it. After leading the Reds in '90, Larkin picked up right where he left off in '91. His .302 average ranked sixth in the NL, along with 20 homers and 69 RBIs — despite missing 39 games with a variety of nicks and scrapes.

Outfield
BARRY BONDS
PITTSBURGH PIRATES

When the joy of summer (and a second straight NL East title for the Pirates) died in October, thoughts in Pittsburgh turned to '92. Hottest on the rumor mill: The new season would be Barry Bonds's last by the famous Three Rivers or, worse, the Bucs would deal Bonds before the '92 season while he still had a contract.

With all of the other changes in Pittsburgh, the potential loss of Bonds hurts most. The son of superstar Bobby Bonds, Barry has proven to be his dad's equal.

A .292 hitter in '91, Barry's eyes lit up with runners in scoring position. Then his average soared to .345. That helped account for his 116 RBIs, just one off the NL lead. And though he finished up the track in the batting race, he was the easy winner in on-base percentage, thanks to 107 walks, 25 of them intentional.

What's the scout's line on the Buc left fielder? A superb base runner (43 steals) and defensive outfielder, he has power all over the park and hits lefties as well as he does right-handers. If he has a weakness (and it's debatable), it's a high-inside fastball. But pitchers had better be prepared to come inside off the plate, or this guy will murder the ball.

Outfield
ANDRE DAWSON
CHICAGO CUBS

One of the best things that ever happened to the Chicago Cubs was that Andre Dawson hated the artificial turf at Montreal's Olympic Stadium. Given a chance to escape, the Hawk flew off to Chicago, and the Cubs have profited big time!

Now, at age 37, Dawson regularly shakes off the aches and pains to play some of the best right field anywhere. His ability at the plate has never been questioned.

"Years ago," says Dawson, "I learned an important lesson. The Reds' Tony Perez told me to avoid putting pressure on myself. I think I've finally learned to take it easy and have fun on the ball field."

In '91 that translated to a solid .272 season with 31 homers and 104 RBIs, both well among the league leaders. At a time when the Cubbies were flopping around the second division most of the season, Dawson and second sacker Ryne Sandberg were among the few bright spots.

"I'd like another shot at postseason baseball," says the 6–3, 195-pound Dawson. "I wasn't physically sound for the 1989 NL Championship Series. That was probably my biggest disappointment."

With any kind of luck, the rest of the Cubs can help fulfill their Hawk's wish — soon!

Outfield
BOBBY BONILLA
NEW YORK METS

The Mets signing of Pittsburgh's Bobby Bonilla triggered the greatest outburst of cheers and tears in years. The cheers came from Mets fans who saw the hometown boy as the guy who will return their team to the top of the standings. The tears came from Pirates fans and from those who figure they won't be able to afford tickets when the team finally figures out how to pay Bobby Bo's $29 million.

Meanwhile, let's pencil in Bobby on our '92 All-Pro roster, even before manager Jeff Torborg figures out where to play his new-found talent.

Bonilla, who grew up in the Bronx near Yankee Stadium, has become a major threat every time he brings a bat to the plate. A switch-hitter, who hit for a better average against righties and for more power against lefties in '91, Bobby Bo cuts a menacing figure at 6–3, 240 pounds. Pitchers try to bust him inside with fastballs, then try to get him to chase breaking balls low and away.

Despite an excellent .302 batting average in '91, the key for Bonilla is power. Batting ahead of Bobby Bonds, Bo smacked 18 homers and knocked in 100 runs for the Bucs last year.

Catcher
BENITO SANTIAGO
SAN DIEGO PADRES

Almost every National League fan can argue about this choice. The folks in Atlanta, Pittsburgh, St. Louis, and Los Angeles may even have a decent beef. But hard-throwing Benito Santiago remains our choice as the NL's best backstop.

The 27-year-old from Puerto Rico has set the standard for defensive catchers. His arm could legally be classified as a firearm. Once he finally mastered the art of throwing from his knees — thus saving the time needed to stand up and throw, he has been throwing out enemy base stealers nearly 60% of the time. (He doesn't do as well using the conventional method.)

But the key to Santiago's successes in 1991 was good health. After playing in only 100 games in '90 because of a broken arm (courtesy of a misdirected pitch), Benito bounced back to play in 148 games last year, hitting .267 (just above his career average) and knocking in 87 runs, easily a career high. Toss in 17 homers and 22 doubles, and you have an all-star season.

Unlike the typical beefy catcher (read that Mike LaValliere), Santiago is a lean, mean athlete who grew up pitching and playing shortstop. Fact is, Benito tossed nine no-hitters in Little League. Interesting!

TOM GLAVINE
ATLANTA BRAVES

How would the 1991 season have changed if Atlanta left-hander Tommy Glavine had chosen to play hockey instead of baseball in 1984? Drafted by the L.A. Kings, Glavine opted for the Braves, who had picked him in the second round of the baseball selection pool, and the rest is history. Baseball history.

"What a great year '91 was for Glavine," raves his manager, Bobby Cox. "Right from the opener, he was in great form. He had great control most of the time, had excellent velocity on his fastball, a great change, and a solid curve. What else do you want?"

Not much, Skip. But if you throw in leadership on a young staff, you've got it all. Atlanta folks had been talking hopefully about Glavine for several years now. It took his '91 performance — his first 20-win season (20–11), a 2.55 ERA (third in the NL), and nine complete games (tying for the league lead) — to make believers out of them and earn him the Cy Young award.

Glavine was one of the keys to Atlanta's worst-to-first miracle. He won 10 road games in '91, equaling his victory total home *and* away the previous year. And in a league with no DH, Tom's a plus with his .230 batting average and 15 sacrifice bunts.

26

JOHN SMILEY
PITTSBURGH PIRATES

When the chips were down, Pittsburgh manager Jim Leyland knew what to do. He handed the ball to lefty John Smiley, and nine innings later, the Bucs had a victory.

The ace of what was probably the NL's best pitching staff throughout the '91 season, southpaw Smiley finally rewarded the Pirates' patience with a spectacular season. The Bucs spent a midrange draft pick (12th round) in 1983 to pluck the 6–4, 200-pound Smiley from Perkiomen Valley (PA) High School. It took five years for Smiley to make the big club and another five for him to make it big. Now, at age 27, he looks like the pitcher the Bucs hoped he'd be.

There were questions after the '90 season. A broken hand limited John to only 25 starts, a 9–10 record (with a 4.64 ERA), and a poor postseason performance. But bouncing back in '91, Smiley parlayed great stuff and superb control (only 44 walks in 207⅔ innings) to a 20–8 mark and a sparkling 3.08 ERA. No Buc lefty had won 20 since John Candelaria in 1977. In fact, he opens the 1992 season with a seven-game winning streak, the best of his career.

The rumor mill features reports that free agents will soon strip the Bucs of much of their talent. They'd be wise to keep Smiley.

An AL-leading .341 bat mark in '91 made Texas 2B Julio Franco the target of every general manager who phoned the Rangers.

American League
TEAM PREVIEWS

AL East
BOSTON RED SOX
1991 Finish: Second (tied)
1992 Prediction: First

Jody Reed

Carlos Quintana

It's the biggest "if" in baseball. If the Red Sox pitching holds up, this club can challenge in the AL East again in '92. But it's only one of the ifs hounding the Sox.

If new manager Butch Hobson can get this sleeping club stirred up, it will be a major help. The Sox were simply too comfortable last year. If Roger Clemens (18–10, 2.62, 241 strikeouts) stays healthy, Hobson's job will be easier. With the addition of ex-Met Frank Viola and surprising Joe Hesketh (12–4, 3.29) back into the fold, the pressure should ease. If youngsters like righty Mike Gardiner (9–10) and lefty Kevin Morton (6–5) blossom this season, so much the better. If Matt Young (3–7) or Danny Darwin (3–6) regain the winning touch, Hobson can be manager of the year. If Jeff Reardon (1–4, 40 saves) remains effective in '92, the bullpen will be in good shape.

There are fewer ifs in the infield, where future Hall-of-Fame 3B Wade Boggs (.332) anchors a solid group. 1B Carlos Quintana (.295, 11 homers, 71 RBIs, and an excellent glove) is set for the foreseeable future, with Jody Reed (.283) and Luis Rivera (.258) a more-than-adequate DP combo. Boston awaits word on the condition of SS Tim Naehring (.109), out since last August with back miseries.

The ifs really crank up in the Boston outfield, where the arrival of Phil Plantier (.331 and 11 homers in only 53 games after an August 9 recall) made folks like Mike Greenwell (.300, 83 RBIs), Ellis Burks (.251, 56 RBIs), and Tom Brunansky (.229, 16 homers, 70 RBIs) expendable. Mo Vaughn (.260) should move right in. DH Jack Clark (.249, 28 homers, 87 RBIs) is among the AL's best in that department. Cs Tony Pena (.231) and John Marzano (.263) are fine.

STAT LEADERS — 1991

BATTING
Average: Boggs, .332
Runs: Boggs, 93
Hits: Boggs, 181
Doubles: Boggs, Reed, 42
Triples: Greenwell, 6
Home runs: Clark, 28
RBIs: Clark, 87
Stolen bases: Greenwell, 15

PITCHING
Wins: Clemens, 18
Losses: Harris, 12
Complete games:
    Clemens, 13
Shutouts: Clemens, 4*
Saves: Reardon, 40
Walks: Harris, 69
Strikeouts: Clemens, 241*

*Led league.

AL East
DETROIT TIGERS
1991 Finish: Second (tied)
1992 Prediction: Second

Bill Gullickson   **Milt Cuyler**

"We're still a year away," says Tigers manager Sparky Anderson, as he points his club toward the 1993 AL East race. Some folks still believe, however, that Sparky's gang can do damage in '92.

The Tigers, who finished seven games behind the champion Blue Jays last season, feature a much-improved defense and some outstanding young talent. What's lacking? Sparky's club strikes out too much, his bullpen doesn't strike out enough, and his starters have gotten old in a hurry.

CF Milt Cuyler, one of the AL's top rookies in '91, was at the center of the club's major improvement. The speedy Cuyler hit .257 and stole 41 bases. He has the green light anytime he wants to go. With Rob Deer (.179, 175 strikeouts) probably gone, IF Tony

Phillips (.284) likely goes to left.

Young 3B Travis Fryman (.259, 36 doubles, 91 RBIs) provides the foundation of the infield of tomorrow. Still, Alan Trammell (.248) and Lou Whitaker (.279) may well continue at short and second, at least for a while longer. 1B Cecil Fielder (.261, 44 homers, 133 major-league-leading RBIs) provides all the sock any club might need. He's still stewing about the MVP award he could well have won. C Mickey Tettleton (.263, 89 RBIs) should be back.

Can Bill Gullickson (20–9) possibly improve on his '91 performance? Probably not, but he only needs to come close. More important, how much longer will Frank Tanana (13–12) and Walt Terrell (12–14) pitch at top level? Other pitching questions: Can Detroit find a set-up man for closer Mike Henneman (10–2, 21 saves in 24 chances), and will Mark Leiter (9–7) keep up the pace he set late last season?

STAT LEADERS — 1991

BATTING
Average: Phillips, .284
Runs: Fielder, 102
Hits: Fielder, 163
Doubles: Fryman, 36
Triples: Cuyler, 7
Home runs: Fielder, 44**
RBIs: Fielder, 133*
Stolen bases: Cuyler, 41

PITCHING
Wins: Gullickson, 20**
Losses: Terrell, 14
Complete games:
  Terrell, 8
Shutouts: Terrell,
  Tanana, 2
Saves: Henneman, 21
Walks: Terrell, 79
Strikeouts: Tanana, 107

*Led league.
**Tied for league lead.

AL East
TORONTO BLUE JAYS
1991 Finish: First
1992 Prediction: Third

Devon White   **Roberto Alomar**

In '92, as in most recent springs, the Blue
Jays have the AL East's best talent. Trouble
is, they still have to play the games on the
field, which is often Toronto's undoing. After
a '91 season that saw manager Cito Gaston
leading the club's disabled list (bad back),
the Jays try for back-to-back titles with
enough people to get the job done.

Gaston starts with one of the finest
defensive units in the game. No 2B in recent
memory has the range of Roberto Alomar
(.295, 69 RBIs, 53 steals), who made the
switch from the NL to the AL with great ease.
1B John Olerud, handed the job when Fred
McGriff was dealt to San Diego, hit .256 with
a career-high 17 homers. 3B Kelly Gruber
(.252, 20 homers) plays the hot corner like a
wild man, while SS Manuel Lee (.234) makes

all the big plays defensively with quick hands and feet.

RF Joe Carter (.273, 33 homers, 108 RBIs) is the Blue Jay who makes things happen. His partner, CF Devon White, who owns a pair of baseball's fastest feet, surprised more than a few folks with his club-record 110 runs scored, 181 hits, 40 doubles, and 10 triples. Look for rookie Devon Bell to get a shot in the outfield this year. Neither catcher, Pat Borders or Greg Myers, is top caliber.

Pitching should continue to be the Jays' strong suit with the addition of World Series hero Jack Morris. Surprising rookie Juan Guzman (10–3, 2.99) returns, along with Jimmy Key (16–12), Todd Stottlemyre (15–8), and Dave Wells (15–10, 3.72). Free-agent Tom Candiotti (13–13, 2.65) signed with the Dodgers. The picture gets even better if ace Dave Stieb (out last season after May 22) and reliever Tom Henke (shoulder tendinitis) are back and healthy. If Henke, who's first-rate, doesn't bounce back, Duane Ward leads the pen staff.

STAT LEADERS — 1991

BATTING
Average: Alomar, .295
Runs: White, 110
Hits: Alomar, 188
Doubles: Carter, 42
Triples: Alomar, 11
Home runs: Carter, 33
RBIs: Carter, 108
Stolen bases: Alomar, 53

PITCHING
Wins: Key, 16
Losses: Candiotti, 13
Complete games:
    Candiotti, 6
Shutouts: Key, 2
Saves: Henke, 32
Walks: Stottlemyre, 75
Strikeouts: Ward, 132

AL East
BALTIMORE ORIOLES
1991 Finish: Sixth
1992 Prediction: Fourth

Mike Devereaux

Joe Orsulak

Maybe the best news for Baltimore is that the club's gorgeous new Oriole Park at Camden Yards has a friendly, short porch in right field. That's an open invitation for powerful lefty DH Sam Horn to add to his 23-homer total in '91.

After yo-yoing up and down the AL East standings for the last four years, the Birds are still looking for pitching that will take them back to the top of the heap and leave them there for a while.

Of course, the news isn't all bad when SS Cal Ripken (.323, 34 homers, 114 RBIs), the AL's MVP in '91, is in your lineup every day. As the '92 season opens, Cal has started 1,573 straight games and now stands only 3½ years away from Lou Gehrig's seemingly unreachable total of 2,130 in a row.

Brother Bill Ripken (.216) and Juan Bell should split time at 2B, with a re-signed Glenn Davis, hopefully healthy, at 1B. 3B Leo Gomez (.233) took over from Craig Worthington in May and led all ML rookies with 16 HRs.

Slugging Chito Martinez (.269, 13 HRs, after his July 5 debut) should join Mike Devereaux (.260), Joe Orsulak (.278), and Brady Anderson (.230) in the O's outfield, with rookie Luis Mercedes ready for a full shot this spring. C Chris Hoiles (.243) doesn't threaten to get any Hall-of-Fame votes in the near future.

But pitching is the No. 1 problem. Once you get past Bob Milacki (who led the club with 10 wins) and returning Storm Davis, the staff is barely old enough to shave. But if Mike Mussina and Arthur Rhodes are for real, the O's will begin to rise again. The bullpen (set-up men Jim Poole and Todd Frohwirth; closer Gregg Olson) is better than average. The biggest question: Any hope for Ben McDonald (6–8, 4.84)?

STAT LEADERS — 1991

BATTING
Average: C. Ripken, .323
Runs: C. Ripken, 99
Hits: C. Ripken, 210
Doubles: C. Ripken, 46
Triples: Devereaux, 10
Home runs: C. Ripken, 34
RBIs: C. Ripken, 114
Stolen bases: Devereaux, 16

PITCHING
Wins: Milacki, 10
Losses: Ballard, 12
Complete games:
　Milacki, 3
Shutouts: Mesa, Milacki, 1
Saves: Olson, 31
Walks: Mesa, 62
Strikeouts: Milacki, 108

AL East
MILWAUKEE BREWERS
1991 Finish: Fourth
1992 Prediction: Fifth

Chris Bosio

B.J. Surhoff

Surprise: The Brewers won 83 games in '91 and finished a strong fourth. Surprise: The Brewers canned manager Tom Trebelhorn after the season. (Crime: He was too nice.) *No* surprise: New field boss Phil Garner is one tough customer. Good luck, gentlemen.

Last year's 40–19 finish is cause for hope. Then there's the starting pitching, which is even more hopeful. Big right-hander Chris Bosio (14–10, 3.25) led the charge in the final two months of '91. The quartet is completed by Jaime Navarro (15–12, 3.92), Bill Wegman (15–7, 2.84), and Cal Eldred (2–0 in three late-season starts). Unfortunately, all of them throw right-handed. The necessary lefty could be longtime reliever Dan Plesac (2–7, 8 saves), if righty Doug Henry

(2–1, 1.00, 15 saves) can handle the closer's role. Ex-Phil Bruce Ruffin may help.

2B Willie Randolph had a miracle season (.327, more than 50 points better than his career average) but probably won't be back. Who will play 2B? Was top flop 1B Franklin Stubbs's .213 and 11-homer season an accident? Those are key questions. If Stubbs stumbles again, look for John Jaha (.344, 30 homers at El Paso) to get a shot. Bill Spiers (.283) should be back at short, with Jim Gantner (.283) at third, unless Gary Sheffield (will he be around?) bounces back.

Ageless (he's actually 36) CF Robin Yount (.260, 77 RBIs) should get his 3,000th major-league hit around the All-Star break. Greg Vaughn (.244, 98 RBIs) and Dante Bichette (.238) should surround him again. B.J. Surhoff (.289) is the main backstop until rookie Dave Nilsson is ready. And if there's a better DH than Paul Molitor (.325, 216 hits, 13 triples, 75 RBIs), we haven't spotted him.

STAT LEADERS — 1991

BATTING
Average: Randolph, .327
Runs: Molitor, 133*
Hits: Molitor, 216*
Doubles: Molitor, 32
Triples: Molitor, 13**
Home runs: Vaughn, 27
RBIs: Vaughn, 98
Stolen bases: Molitor, 19

*Led league.
**Tied for league lead.

PITCHING
Wins: Navarro,
    Wegman, 15
Losses: Navarro, 12
Complete games:
    Navarro, 10
Shutouts: Navarro,
    Wegman, 2
Saves: Henry, 15
Walks: Navarro, 73
Strikeouts: Bosio, 117

AL East
NEW YORK YANKEES
1991 Finish: Fifth
1992 Prediction: Sixth

Matt Nokes   **Scott Sanderson**

When '91 Yankee manager Stump Merrill was swept out of office after the season, his coaching staff, including third-base traffic cop Buck Showalter, went with him. Three weeks later, young Buck, with no major-league managing experience, was back as the latest Yankee field boss.

Buck knows the job ahead of him. For the first time in recent memory, the Yankees can actually point with pride at their pitching. The arms are young and need experience, but there is a foundation, at last. Lefty Jeff Johnson (6–11, 5.95) and righties Scott Kamieniecki (4–4, 3.90) and Wade Taylor (7–12, 6.27) should be around for quite a while. Veteran right-hander Scott Sanderson (16–10, 3.81) was outstanding. Reliever John Habyan (4–2, 2.30) pitched very well all year, while closer Steve Farr (5–5, 2.19, 23 saves) is OK.

The left side of the infield should give Showalter a few gray hairs by the end of his rookie season. With any luck, the Yanks will have filled their third-base hole by the time they reach the Bronx in April. Pat Kelly (.242) may not be the answer. At short, Alvaro Espinosa (.256) has worn out his welcome (21 errors). Steve Sax (.304) is a total pro at second, and a less-powerful 1B Don Mattingly (.288) is still a constant threat at the plate and a solid glove man.

Despite a bad back last September, Mel Hall (.285, 80 RBIs, career-high 19 homers) is the solid leader of the outfield. Roberto Kelly (.267) and Bernie Williams (.238) may be two of the few untouchable Yankees. Jesse Barfield, Mike Humphreys, and Gerald Williams join the battle for outfield playing time. C Matt Nokes (.268, 24 homers, 77 RBIs) returned to his rookie form; back-up John Ramos may be ready to help.

STAT LEADERS — 1991

BATTING
Average: Sax, .304
Runs: Sax, 85
Hits: Sax, 198
Doubles: Sax, 38
Triples: P. Kelly,
   Williams, 4
Home runs: Nokes, 24
RBIs: Hall, 80
Stolen bases: R. Kelly, 32

PITCHING
Wins: Sanderson, 16
Losses: Taylor, 12
Complete games:
   Sanderson, 2
Shutouts: Sanderson, 2
Saves: Farr, 23
Walks: Plunk, 62
Strikeouts:
   Sanderson, 130

AL East
CLEVELAND INDIANS
1991 Finish: Seventh
1992 Prediction: Seventh

Felix Fermin

Carlos Baerga

Cleveland manager Mike Hargrove has paid his dues. He has a contract to run the ball club through this '92 season. It isn't long enough.

The '91 Indians made 149 errors (to lead the AL). The '91 Indians failed to score in 18 games and had the AL's lowest on-base percentage. Those things don't go away overnight. But believe it or not, there is hope, though it's long-range hope.

If C Sandy Alomar (.217, only 51 games) gets his banged-up shoulder back into shape, he can be the AL's best. 1B Reggie Jefferson (.198) has plenty of room for improvement. 2B Carlos Baerga hit .288 (a personal best) and could do better. SS Mark Lewis (.264, after hitting .400 in his first major-league month) could be ready to unseat Felix Fermin (.262). 3B Jim Thome (.255 in 27 late-season games) could be ready to go soon.

The outfield should be set with surprising ex-Blue Jay Mark Whiten (.243), hard-to-handle Albert Belle (.282, 28 homers, 95 RBIs), and Alex Cole (.295, 27 team-leading steals). Glenallen Hill (.258) and ex-Astro Kenny Lofton should find a spot somewhere.

Sounds good? You bet. But after that come the Indians' three greatest needs: pitching, pitching, and pitching. Greg Swindell (9–16, 3.48) was about the best the Tribe had last year. But when he refused a contract extension, he was dealt to Cincinnati for a trio of arms. Two of the ex-Reds, Scott Scudder and Jack Armstrong, move right into the Cleveland rotation, now led by Charles Nagy (10–15, 4.13) and Eric King (6–11, 4.60). With one-time ace closer Doug Jones (4–8) gone, set-up man Shawn Hillegas (3–4, 4.34) and closer Steve Olin (17 saves) are the key men in what is, at best, a shaky bullpen.

STAT LEADERS — 1991

BATTING
Average: Cole, .295
Runs: Baerga, 80
Hits: Baerga, 171
Doubles: Belle, 31
Triples: Whiten, 7
Home runs: Belle, 28
RBIs: Belle, 95
Stolen bases: Cole, 27

PITCHING
Wins: Nagy, 10
Losses: Swindell, 16
Complete games:
   Swindell, 7
Shutouts: Three with 1
Saves: Olin, 17
Walks: Nagy, 66
Strikeouts: Swindell, 169

AL West
CHICAGO WHITE SOX
1991 Finish: Second
1992 Prediction: First

Jack McDowell   **Frank Thomas**

Now that the White Sox have opened their beautiful new ball yard on the south side of Chicago, they're ready to fly a flag. With some consistent pitching, it could happen in '92. What's strange, of course, is that the Sox let manager Jeff Torborg take a hike.

Meanwhile, the Chicago cupboard is well stocked. DH Frank Thomas (.318, 32 homers, 109 RBIs) is the toast of the town. 1B Dan Pasqua has re-signed with Chicago, but Thomas may spend more time at first. On the opposite side, 3B Robin Ventura (.284, 23 homers, 100 RBIs) has become one of the league's best. SS Ozzie Guillen (.273, 21 steals) owns a solid glove. There could well be changes at 2B where Scott Fletcher (.206) had become too expensive.

Though Sammy Sosa (.203) bombed in the

Chicago outfield in '91, there were no problems with Lance Johnson (.274, league-lead-tying 13 triples) or Tim Raines (.268, 51 steals). The club could use some help behind the plate where Carlton Fisk (.241) is 44. Ron Karkovice (.246) is fairly decent.

So there's nothing wrong with the Chisox hitting, power, speed, or defense. The problem? It's the same old song: pitching. The starters aren't bad. In fact, Jack McDowell (17–10, 3.41) is excellent, and righty Alex Fernandez (9–13, 4.51) and lefty Greg Hibbard (11–11, 4.31) show flashes of brilliance. Ancient knuckleballer Charlie Hough (he's 44, too) still gets the job done. Trouble is, the group just isn't consistent. Lefty Wilson Alvarez (3–2, 3.51, and a no-hitter in his first White Sox start) and right-ies Roberto Hernandez and Ramon Garcia are ready to bloom in '92. Set-up man Scott Radinsky (5–5, 2.02) usually delivers the lead to closer Bobby Thigpen (7–5, 30 saves).

STAT LEADERS — 1991

BATTING
Average: Thomas, .318
Runs: Thomas, 104
Hits: Thomas, 178
Doubles: Thomas, 31
Triples: Johnson, 13**
Home runs: Thomas, 32
RBIs: Thomas, 109
Stolen bases: Raines, 51

PITCHING
Wins: McDowell, 17
Losses: Fernandez, 13
Complete games:
    McDowell, 15*
Shutouts: McDowell, 3
Saves: Thigpen, 30
Walks: Hough, 94
Strikeouts: McDowell, 191

*Led league.
**Tied for league lead.

AL West
TEXAS RANGERS
1991 Finish: Third
1992 Prediction: Second

Juan Gonzales

Rafael Palmeiro

You'll have to look far and wide to find an American League pitcher who relishes facing the Texas Rangers lineup. Trouble is, the Rangers' pitchers don't do much with the enemy attackers, either.

Texas hit .270, third in the AL in '91, led by AL bat king 2B Julio Franco (.341, 15 homers). But he was hardly the only threat. 1B Rafael Palmeiro (.322) led the majors in doubles (49) and was second in total bases (336). Dean Palmer (.187, 15 homers) took over at 3B after Steve Buechele was traded last August 30, with light-hitting Jeff Huson at SS.

The outfield is even tougher. Ruben Sierra (.307, 25 HRs, and 116 RBIs, third in the AL) leads the way along with Juan Gonzalez (.264, 27 homers, 102 RBIs). Gary Pettis (.216),

46

who gets to everything in center, had 29 steals. DH Brian Downing (.278, 17 homers) will be back, so the Rangers have plenty of depth here. In 81 games beginning June 19, rookie Ivan Rodriguez (.264) showed that he's a future All-Star. C Geno Petralli was signed for another season.

Then there's the pitching. Ugh! Future Hall-of-Famer Nolan Ryan (12–6, 2.91, 203 strikeouts in only 173 innings) continues to amaze everyone who sees him pitch. But he's 45, and who knows if he'll get old overnight.

The ace of the squad turned out to be Jose Guzman (13–7, 3.08) who had missed two seasons with injuries. The expected aces, right-handers Kevin Brown (9–12, 4.40) and Bobby Witt (3–7, an incredible 6.09!), didn't do a thing. Hector Fajardo (0–2), who came from Pittsburgh in the Buechele trade, could help in '92. The rest of the young starters are a year or so away. The bullpen, led by super-closer Jeff Russell (6–4, 30 saves), is just fine.

STAT LEADERS — 1991

BATTING

Average: Franco, .341*
Runs: Palmeiro, 115
Hits: Palmeiro, Sierra, 203
Doubles: Palmeiro, 49*
Triples: Pettis, Sierra, 5
Home runs: Gonzalez, 27
RBIs: Sierra, 116
Stolen bases: Franco, 36

*Led league.

PITCHING

Wins: Guzman, 13
Losses: Brown, 12
Complete games:
    Guzman, 5
Shutouts: Ryan, 2
Saves: Russell, 30
Walks: Brown, 90
Strikeouts: Ryan, 203

AL West
OAKLAND ATHLETICS
1991 Finish: Fourth
1992 Prediction: Third

Terry Steinbach   **Mark McGwire**

While the Minnesota Twins were busy going from worst to first last year, the "Dynasty" Athletics were doing the improbable: becoming just another ball club. The 84–78 record wasn't horrible; the fourth-place finish was.

It can't happen again — maybe. It took off-years by practically everyone in manager Tony LaRussa's lineup to sink the A's ship. If just a few bounce back, so will the team — unless the pitching woes continue.

Only an early vacation kept 1B Mark McGwire (.201, but 22 homers and 75 RBIs) from sinking beneath the famous Mendoza line (below-.200 batting average). Ron Witmeyer may be ready to help here. 2B Mike Gallego was superb while the club collapsed. His .247 average wasn't bad; his 12 homers exceeded his previous five-year total. It must get better at short where Walt Weiss (.226) missed the last 109 games. Mike Bordick (.238) filled in nicely, but isn't a long-term answer. When Carney Lansford missed the season, his replacements didn't get it done. If Carney isn't healthy, rookie Scott Hemond might get the call.

RF Jose Canseco (.266, 44 homers, 122 RBIs), CF Dave Henderson (.276, 25 homers, 85 RBIs), and DH Harold Baines (.295, 20 homers, 90 RBIs) had outstanding years, but Rickey Henderson (.268, 58 steals) didn't. C Terry Steinbach (.274) is among the best.

But the pitching is the big question. Can Dave Stewart (11–11, 5.18), Bob Welch (12–13, 4.58), and relief ace Dennis Eckersley (5–4, but 43 saves) return to championship form? If not, it's Mike Moore (17–8, 2.96) and a bunch of guys waiting for upcoming stars Bruce Walton and Todd Van Poppel.

STAT LEADERS — 1991

BATTING
Average: Baines, .295
Runs: Canseco, 115
Hits: D. Henderson, 158
Doubles: D. Henderson, 33
Triples: Three with 4
Home runs: Canseco, 44**
RBIs: Canseco, 122
Stolen bases:
   R. Henderson, 58*

PITCHING
Wins: Moore, 17
Losses: Welch, 13
Complete games:
   Welch, 7
Shutouts: Three with 1
Saves: Eckersley, 43
Walks: Stewart,
   Moore, 105
Strikeouts: Moore, 153

 *Led league.
**Tied for league lead.

49

AL West
CALIFORNIA ANGELS
1991 Finish: Seventh
1992 Prediction: Fourth

Jim Abbott

Mark Langston

Told that the California Angels, who finished 81–81, were the best last-place team in baseball history, left-hander Chuck Finley quickly snapped: "I'd rather be on the worst first-place team!"

Making up the 14 games that separated the Angels from first place won't be easy. The pitching doesn't figure to get any better. California had three of the AL's top winners in lefties Finley (18–9, 3.80), Jim Abbott (18–11, 2.89), and Mark Langston (19–8, 3.00). New manager Buck Rodgers can't ask for more than that. Even his bullpen is in great shape, with classy set-up man Mark Eichhorn (3–3, 1.98) and the AL's new closer-king, right-hander Bryan Harvey (2–4, 46 league-leading saves, a 1.60 ERA, and a 6-to-1 strikeouts-to-walks ratio).

Rodgers's boss, ex-Cardinal manager Whitey Herzog, likes ball clubs that can run but, except for LF Luis Polonia (.296, 48 steals), there's no speed to be found. Expect lots of tinkering. Free-agent 1B Wally Joyner (.301, 21 homers) left for K.C. If rookie Lee Stevens replaces him at 1B, ex-Phil Von Hayes will go to the OF. 2B Luis Sojo (.258) is scheduled to return, along with 3B Gary Gaetti (.246, 18 homers). Gary DiSarcina, who improved his offense in AAA, should get a shot to replace Dick Schofield (.225) at short.

With Dave Winfield gone, there's a hole in the outfield. Junior Felix (.283) can do it, if he stays healthy. He played only 66 games between trips to the DL last year and has never played more than 127 games in a season. Ex-Met Hubie Brooks and Max Venable (.246) should see plenty of action.

With Lance Parrish's (.216) best years behind him, John Orton (.203 in a late trial) is the catcher of tomorrow.

STAT LEADERS — 1991

BATTING
Average: Joyner, .301
Runs: Polonia, 92
Hits: Polonia, 179
Doubles: Joyner, 34
Triples: Polonia, 8
Home runs: Winfield, 28
RBIs: Joyner, 96
Stolen bases: Polonia, 48

PITCHING
Wins: Langston, 19
Losses: McCaskill, 19*
Complete games:
 Langston, 7
Shutouts: Finley, 2
Saves: Harvey, 46*
Walks: Finley, 101
Strikeouts: Langston, 183

*Led league.

AL West
MINNESOTA TWINS
1991 Finish: First
1992 Prediction: Fifth

Chuck Knoblauch   **Kevin Tapani**

Here we go again. The Twins are champions of the world, without winning a World Series road game. They've got the talent to win again, but manager Tom Kelly would be a lot more comfortable if his club would learn to win away from home.

The pitching is good and can get better. Though Jack Morris (18–12, 3.43) was an off-season free agent and signed with Toronto, the Twins have plenty of other talent. Right-handers Kevin Tapani (16–9, 2.99, great stuff and pinpoint control) and Scott Erickson (20–8, 3.18, despite arm and elbow injuries) are becoming dominant pitchers. David West (4–4, 4.54) is a wonderful set-up man, and when the ball goes to closer Rick Aguilera (4–5, 42 saves), the game is usually in the bank. With some experience, lefty Denny Neagle and righty Willie Banks are almost ready.

Slick-fielding SS Greg Gagne (.265) is the glue holding the infield together. Top rookie 2B Chuck Knoblauch (.281, club-leading 25 steals) was a pleasant '91 surprise, with expanding 1B Kent Hrbek (.284, 89 RBIs), 3B Scott Leius (who started hitting in the last half of '91), and World Series hero 3B Mike Pagliarulo (if he stays) anchoring the group.

Brian Harper (.311, 69 RBIs) is the AL's best hitting catcher but is just average defensively. Watch for Lenny Webster to get a thorough look this spring.

All-everything CF Kirby Puckett (.319, 89 RBIs) remains one of the most productive (and exciting) players in the game. LF Dan Gladden (.247) is too expensive for a lead-off hitter with a .306 on-base average. Shane Mack (.310) was spectacular in the second half. DH Chili Davis (.277, 29 homers, 93 RBIs) was one of the league's best. Rookies Jarvis Brown and Pedro Munoz are comers.

STAT LEADERS — 1991

BATTING
Average: Puckett, .319
Runs: Puckett, 92
Hits: Puckett, 195
Doubles: Davis, 34
Triples: Gladden, 9
Home runs: Davis, 29
RBIs: Davis, 93
Stolen bases: Knoblauch, 25

PITCHING
Wins: Erickson, 20*
Losses: Morris, 12
Complete games:
    Morris, 10
Shutouts: Erickson, 3
Saves: Aguilera, 42
Walks: Morris, 92
Strikeouts: Morris, 163

*Tied for league lead.

AL West
KANSAS CITY ROYALS
1991 Finish: Sixth
1992 Prediction: Sixth

Kevin Appier   Brian McRae

For a club that floundered in '91, the Royals aren't in bad shape. While most everyone in baseball is looking for pitching, Kansas City was so comfortable with its mound staff that it used its arms to buy bats. It's a shortage of run production that kept the Royals near the bottom of the West last year, and that problem may be over.

Manager Hal McRae, who steered Kaycee to a 66–58 mark after becoming the boss last May 24, looks to his veteran mound crew to get things going. Most of the pitching comes from the right side, including Mark Gubicza (9–12, 5.68), Mike Boddicker (12–12, 4.08), Kevin Appier (13–10, 3.42), and Flash Gordon (9–14, 3.87), though K.C. all-timer Bret Saberhagen went to the Mets. Mark Davis (6–3, 4.45) will likely be the left-handed starter. The bullpen is in excellent shape with Joel Johnston (1–0, 0.40) and Jeff Montgomery (4–4, 33 saves).

The infield defense is solid when Terry Shumpert (.217) is at second and David Howard (.216) at short, though ex-Met Gregg Jefferies is a liability at 3B. Ex-Angel Wally Joyner (.301, 21 homers) will get most of the action at first. The major question mark: longtime superstar George Brett, now the DH, turns 39 in May, and slumped from .329 to .255 last season. Is this the end?

With Danny Tartabull (.316, 31 homers, 100 RBIs) gone, steady ex-Met Kevin McReynolds should step in — and up. Manager McRae's son, Brian, stole 20 bases and knocked in 64 runs while switch-hitting .261 in '91. He's a comer. Kirk Gibson (.236, 16 homers) has slipped badly.

Catching is in good hands with Mike MacFarlane (.277, 41 RBIs), Brent Mayne (.251, 31 RBIs), and ex-Oriole Bob Melvin (.250, 23 RBIs).

STAT LEADERS — 1991

BATTING

Average: Tartabull, .316
Runs: McRae, 86
Hits: McRae, 164
Doubles: Brett, 40
Triples: McRae, 9
Home runs: Tartabull, 31
RBIs: Tartabull, 100
Stolen bases: McRae, 20

PITCHING

Wins: Saberhagen,
    Appier, 13
Losses: Gordon, 14
Complete games:
    Saberhagen, 7
Shutouts: Appier, 3
Saves: Montgomery, 33
Walks: Gordon, 87
Strikeouts: Gordon, 167

AL West
SEATTLE MARINERS
1991 Finish: Fifth
1992 Prediction: Seventh

Randy Johnson   **Edgar Martinez**

Imaginary TV commercial:

Voice: Hey, Jim Lefebvre, you just managed the Seattle Mariners to their first winning season. The club drew its all-time record attendance. They set lots of new club marks. So what are you going to do now?

Lefebvre: I'm going to Chicago!

That's about it. After leading the M's to their best campaign, Jim was fired. (A month later, he wound up as the new Cubs manager.) The new occupant of the hot seat in Seattle is Bill Plummer, who finds some talent, more problems, and the threat of a sale or move to Florida hanging over the club.

There's no money to operate in Seattle, a major hang-up. That's why the team's No. 1 superstar, Ken Griffey, Jr. (.327, 22 homers,

100 RBIs), got little protection at the plate until ex-Giant slugger Kevin Mitchell arrived. Outfield mate Jay Buhner (.244, 27 homers) is more than adequate.

1B Pete O'Brien (.248, 88 RBIs) shocked a few folks with his excellent glove. 3B Edgar Martinez (.307, 14 homers) has stepped up among the AL's best at the hot corner. The middle pair, 2B Harold Reynolds (.254) and SS Omar Vizquel (.230), are holding their own. Catching is a problem; the club isn't good enough to carry disappointing Dave Valle (.194).

Pitching will be adequate so long as right-hander Brian Holman (13–14, 3.69) is healthy. Huge (he's 6–10) Randy Johnson (13–10, 3.98, 228 strikeouts) still frightens rival hitters. Erik Hanson was 8–8 last year despite a tender elbow. Bill Krueger (11–8, 3.60), a free agent, will likely be back. With Bill Swift (17 saves) and Mike Jackson (7–7, 14 saves) dealt to SF for Mitchell, the bullpen is a problem.

STAT LEADERS — 1991

BATTING

Average: Griffey, Jr., .327
Runs: Martinez, 98
Hits: Griffey, Jr., 179
Doubles: Griffey, Jr., 42
Triples: Reynolds, 6
Home runs: Buhner, 27
RBIs: Griffey, Jr., 100
Stolen bases: Reynolds, 28

PITCHING

Wins: Holman, Johnson, 13
Losses: Holman, 14
Complete games: Holman, 5
Shutouts: Holman, 3
Saves: Swift, 17
Walks: Johnson, 152*
Strikeouts: Johnson, 228

*Led league.

Smooth-stroking, timely hitting, super-fielding Will "The Thrill" Clark leads the powerful Giants as the NL's All-Pro 1B.

National
League
TEAM PREVIEWS

NL East
NEW YORK METS
1991 Finish: Fifth
1992 Prediction: First

David Cone

Howard Johnson

When the Mets stole Chicago White Sox manager Jeff Torborg to run their club in 1992, they promised to do whatever it took to give him a competitive ball club. An empty promise? Hardly. First, they spent $36 million to put Bobby Bonilla and Eddie Murray into Jeff's lineup, then gambled away three starters (Kevin McReynolds, Gregg Jefferies, and Keith Miller) to acquire K.C. double Cy Young winner Bret Saberhagen and infielder Bill Pecota. Gutsy moves all around. Stupid moves? Only time will tell.

Even with Saberhagen, the pitching scene is shaky. Bret has had arm troubles, of course. Met ace Doc Gooden (13–7, 3.60) and fire-balling lefty Sid Fernandez (1–3, 2.86) are returning from winter surgery, always a questionable deal. NL strikeout king David Cone (14–14, 3.29, 241 Ks) must become a more dominant pitcher.

The bullpen remains in the left arm of John Franco (5–9, 30 saves) with improvement needed from the set-up men. Huge (6–9) ex-basketball star Terry Bross is ready to help in the pen, with Anthony Young getting a full shot as a starter.

The off-season additions should help the offense, which flopped in '91. Now, finally, NL homer and RBI king RF Howard Johnson (.259, 38 homers, 117 RBIs) gets help from LF Bonilla and 1B Murray. Dave Magadan (a sorry .258 before dual shoulder surgery) may move to third, with defensive whiz Kevin Elster at short. Rookie Chris Donnells gets a full look at third, with Pecota likely to get the call at second. But it will take improvement from CF Vincent Coleman (.255, 37 steals in 72 games) to take the club over the top. Promising rookie Todd Hundley does the catching.

STAT LEADERS — 1991

BATTING
Average: Jefferies, .272
Runs: Johnson, 108
Hits: Johnson, 146
Doubles: Johnson, 34
Triples: Coleman, 5
Home runs: Johnson, 38*
RBIs: Johnson, 117*
Stolen bases: Coleman, 37

PITCHING
Wins: Cone, 14
Losses: Viola, 15
Complete games: Cone, 5
Shutouts: Cone, 2
Saves: Franco, 30
Walks: Cone, 73
Strikeouts: Cone, 241*

*Led league.

NL East
CHICAGO CUBS
1991 Finish: Fourth
1992 Prediction: Second

George Bell   **Mark Grace**

The Cubs' 1991 season, which began with
so much hope, finished in confusion. Within
weeks after the season ended, they had no
president, no manager (Jim Lefebvre got the
job), and a major rebuilding job.

The problems begin with pitching. Staff
ace Greg Maddux (15–11, 3.35) is just fine.
His 37 starts led the league. Ex-Dodger Mike
Morgan provides instant help. The rest of the
crowd is just so-so. Shawn Boskie (4–9) and
Frank Castillo (6–7) are the best of the
bunch. Ex-ace Rick Sutcliffe (6–5) will
probably not be back. Danny Jackson (1–5
between disabled-list visits), the expensive one, is the biggest question of all. The
healthy return of Mike Harkey will help big-
time. The 1991 closer, Dave Smith, went
0–6 with a 6.00 ERA (despite 17 saves). Paul

Assenmacher (7–8, 15 saves) was better.

The rest of the club is in better shape. Start with All-Pro 2B Ryne Sandberg (.291, 100 RBIs, 26 homers, super defense). A major item on the Chicago off-season agenda was signing Ryne beyond 1992. It will cost plenty. The rest of the infield is superb on defense, reasonable on offense. 1B Mark Grace (.273) remains a constant threat. 3B is a problem, where Luis Salazar (.258) was a free agent. SS Shawon Dunston (.260), blessed with a cannon for an arm, signed on again, though rookie Rey Sanchez may be ready soon.

The outfield is the team's centerpiece. All-Pro Andre Dawson (.272, 31 homers, 104 RBIs) joins past All-Pro George Bell (.285, 86 RBIs, 15 homers). Center field could be a problem; Jerome Walton (.219) certainly isn't the answer. The catching corps is in even worse shape.

Look for righty Turk Wendell and lefties Lance Dickson and Yorkis Perez to get a shot at mound spots this spring.

STAT LEADERS — 1991

BATTING
Average: Sandberg, .291
Runs: Sandberg, 104
Hits: Sandberg, 170
Doubles: Sandberg, 32
Triples: Dunston, 7
Home runs: Dawson, 31
RBIs: Dawson, 104
Stolen bases: Landrum, 27

PITCHING
Wins: Maddux, 15
Losses: Maddux, Bielecki, 11
Complete games: Maddux, 7
Shutouts: Maddux, 2
Saves: Smith, 17
Walks: Maddux, 66
Strikeouts: Maddux, 198

NL East
PITTSBURGH PIRATES
1991 Finish: First
1992 Prediction: Third

Andy Van Slyke   **Jay Bell**

If the federal government could step in to
help the money-poor savings & loan banks,
shouldn't it do the same for the Pittsburgh
Pirates? Money is the major problem in Buc-
land, where even the magic of manager Jim
Leyland might not be enough to win a third
straight NL East title.

All-Pro RF Bobby Bonilla (.302, 100 RBIs)
hit the free-agent road to New York. Without Bobby Bo, 1B Orlando Merced (.275) goes
to right, with either injured 3B Jeff King (.239)
or John Wehner (.340 in 37 games) moving
to first. Free-agent 3B Steve Buechele (.246),
an excellent glove man, has re-signed.

LF Bobby Bonds (.292, 116 RBIs, 25 HRs)
enters the final year of his Buc contract and
could be dealt early. But CF Andy Van Slyke
(.265) will hold the outfield together. SS Jay

Bell (.270, 16 homers, 96 runs) returns from a career year, now solid on defense as well. 2B Chico Lind is first-rate. Pittsburgh re-signed C Mike LaValliere (.289); but the rest of the catching is just fair, and there's no help on the farm.

Starting pitching is in fine shape, led by lefty John Smiley (20–8, 3.08). Doug Drabek (15–14, 3.07), lefty Zane Smith (16–10, 3.20), Randy Tomlin (8–7, 2.98), and Bob Walk (9–2, 3.60) complete an outstanding rotation. Bullpen-by-committee should remain the rule in Pittsburgh, paced by Bill Landrum (17 saves) and Stan Belinda (16 saves). Bob Kipper and Neal Heaton, a one-time All-Star, will likely be gone.

The experts said that a 1991 repeat by the Pirates wouldn't happen. They were wrong. They're saying the same in '92, so take your pick. There's no doubt that Leyland is one of the game's top managers, but will that be enough?

STAT LEADERS — 1991

BATTING

Average: Bonilla, .302
Runs: Bonilla, 102
Hits: Bonilla, 174
Doubles: Bonilla, 44*
Triples: Bell, 8
Home runs: Bonds, 25
RBIs: Bonds, 116
Stolen bases: Bonds, 43

PITCHING

Wins: Smiley, 20**
Losses: Drabek, 14
Complete games:
    Smith, 6
Shutouts: Smith, 3
Saves: Landrum, 17
Walks: Drabek, 62
Strikeouts: Drabek, 142

*Led league.
**Tied for league lead.

NL East
ST. LOUIS CARDINALS
1991 Finish: Second
1992 Prediction: Fourth

Lee Smith

Felix Jose

The Cardinals may well have been the NL East's biggest surprise in '91. Figured to finish near the bottom of the division standings, manager Joe Torre's Redbirds finished second, pushing the Pirates most of the way. They could do as well or better in '92.

They still play Cardinal baseball. They have tons of speed and defense, hit for average, enjoy fine starting pitching, own a spectacular closer, and have absolutely no power. Hey, it works, doesn't it?

They moved in the fences at Busch Stadium last fall, so the Cards should get more homer power from Pedro Guerrero, Todd Zeile, and ex-Expo Andres Galarraga. There's also a bunch of talent all over the field, including outfielders Ray Lankford

(.251, 69 RBIs, 44 steals) and Felix Jose (.305, 77 RBIs, 20 steals). Versatile 2B Jose Oquendo (.240) should be back, along with future Hall-of-Fame SS Ozzie Smith (.285). If Zeile goes to first, look for Stan Royer to get a shot at third.

Catching is in fine shape. Tom Pagnozzi (.264) tossed out 47% of enemy runners attempting to steal. And young Ray Stephens looks ready to back him up.

If Joe Magrane (elbow problems) is healthy in '92, a fine young pitching staff will become first-rate. Young lefty Omar Olivares (11–7, 3.57, all victories coming after June 28) joins '91 rookie Rheal Cormier (4–5), Jose DeLeon (5–9), Bob Tewksbury (11–12), and Bryn Smith (12–9) in the rotation. Tireless Lee Smith (NL-record 47 saves in only 53 chances, plus a 6–3 record) seemingly can work every night.

The Cards have enough pitching, but they need to score more runs. If they do, an NL East title could happen.

STAT LEADERS — 1991

BATTING
Average: Jose, .305
Runs: O. Smith, 96
Hits: Jose, 173
Doubles: Jose, 40
Triples: Lankford, 15*
Home runs: Zeile, 11
RBIs: Zeile, 81
Stolen bases: Lankford, 44

PITCHING
Wins: B. Smith, 12
Losses: Tewksbury, 12
Complete games:
   B. Smith, Tewksbury, 3
Shutouts: None
Saves: L. Smith, 47*
Walks: Hill, 67
Strikeouts: Hill, 121

*Led league.

NL East
PHILADELPHIA PHILLIES
1991 Finish: Third
1992 Prediction: Fifth

Terry Mulholland

Dale Murphy

Given another shot at managing in the big leagues, Phillies field boss Jim Fregosi finally found his turnaround situation. The Phillies finished as high as third (barely) for the first time since 1986 and may well have left the basement behind for years to come.

Still the Phils don't seem prepared to challenge for the NL East title for a while. There is strong starting pitching from lefty Terry Mulholland (16–13, 3.61) and right-handers Tommy (No-Hit) Greene (13–7, 3.38) and Jose DeJesus (10–9, 3.42). But in a game that requires five starters, the Phillies come up short. Ex-Angel Kyle Abbott (for Von Hayes) could help, and perhaps Tyler Green, in his first full season as a pro, could be ready by the end of the year. Andy Ashby, another right-hander, could win a spot.

The infield is a mixed blessing. 1B John Kruk comes off a spectacular .294 season (with a career-high 21 homers and 92 RBIs), and Dave Hollins seems to be the long-term answer at 3B. Since neither Mickey Morandini nor SS Dickie Thon (lost to free agency) was doing enough, the Phillies brought in well-traveled Mariano Duncan and ex-Brewer Dale Sveum to shore it up.

A healthy Lenny Dykstra (remember his driving misadventures last spring?) means speed, defense, and hitting in CF. If he's right, so are the Phils. Dale Murphy (.252, 81 RBIs) should return in right with Wes Chamberlain (.240, 50 RBIs), the Phils' leading homer and RBI man during the second half of '91, over in left.

Dykstra's passenger last spring, C Darren Daulton, was injured for most of '91 and hit a pitiful .196, simply not enough.

The Phils' picture is brighter, but it's probably not ready for prime time yet.

STAT LEADERS — 1991

BATTING	PITCHING
Average: Kruk, .294	Wins: Mulholland, 16
Runs: Kruk, 84	Losses: Mulholland, 13
Hits: Kruk, 158	Complete games:
Doubles: Murphy, 33	Mulholland, 8
Triples: Kruk, 6	Shutouts: Mulholland, 3
Home runs: Kruk, 21	Saves: Williams, 30
RBIs: Kruk, 92	Walks: DeJesus, 128*
Stolen bases: Dykstra, 24	Strikeouts: Greene, 154

*Led league.

NL East
MONTREAL EXPOS
1991 Finish: Sixth
1992 Prediction: Sixth

Marquis Grissom   **Dennis Martinez**

The big baseball question in Montreal isn't how the Expos will finish the season; it's: Will Olympic Stadium finish the season? Huge chunks of concrete fell from the rafters of the huge ballpark last fall, forcing the sorry Expos to play the final month on the road. Does it get any worse than that?

It shouldn't. Manager Tom Runnells, in his first (and, perhaps, last) full season, can look to decent pitching and a good outfield to make his club competitive.

Start with the outfield combo. LF Ivan Calderon, off a spectacular first NL year (.300, 19 homers, 75 RBIs), anchors a group that includes CF Marquis Grissom (.267, 76 league-leading steals) and RF Larry Walker (.290, 16 homers, 64 RBIs), the future leader of Montreal's power department. In addition, Darren Reed and Moises Alou should bounce back from injuries.

The infield is unsteady. With 1B Andres Galarraga, once an All-Pro, off to St. Louis for P Ken Hill, Calderon may be moved to first to pump up the offense. Unless he's dealt, 2B Delino DeShields (.238) might join youngsters like SS Wil Cordero and Bret Barberie (.353 in 57 games last year). Another former All-Pro, 3B Tim Wallach, could be gone, too.

Young C Greg Colbrunn should get a chance in '92, especially if free-agent Mike Fitzgerald departs.

Dennis (No-Hit) Martinez (14–11) leads a pitching staff with decent potential. Mark (Almost No-Hit) Gardner (9–11), Brian Barnes (5–8), Hill (11–10), and a healthy Chris Nabholz round out the rotation. Leading saver Barry Jones (13 saves) was shipped to Philly (for C Darrin Fletcher), thus leaving a group effort in the pen.

STAT LEADERS — 1991

BATTING
Average: Calderon, .300
Runs: DeShields, 83
Hits: Grissom, 149
Doubles: Walker, 30
Triples: Grissom, 9
Home runs: Calderon, 19
RBIs: Calderon, 75
Stolen bases: Grissom, 76*

*Led league.
**Tied for league lead.

PITCHING
Wins: Martinez, 14
Losses: Martinez, Gardner, 11
Complete games: Martinez, 9**
Shutouts: Martinez, 5*
Saves: Jones, 13
Walks: Barnes, 84
Strikeouts: Martinez, 123

NL West
CINCINNATI REDS
1991 Finish: Fifth
1992 Prediction: First

Paul O'Neill   Jose Rijo

You need to look pretty hard to find a better infield combo than the one Reds manager Lou Piniella pencils onto his lineup card every day. That makes it even more difficult to explain why the 1990 World Champs sank to fifth in the NL West in '91.

1B Hal Morris, a one-time Yankee prospect, hit .318 in his first full season and nearly won an NL batting championship. 2B Bill Doran (.280) proved he's still one of the league's best at the pivot spot. The left side is super strong, with All-Pro SS Barry Larkin (.302, 20 homers) and surprising 3B Chris Sabo (.301, 26 homers, 88 RBIs, all career highs). No other infield does it better.

The outfield is nearly as strong, even though CF Eric Davis (.235, 11 homers, only 89 games) was dealt to L.A. for pitching.

Losing the troubled Davis may turn out to be a blessing. To replace Davis, Cincy dealt excess pitching to San Diego for Bip Roberts and to Montreal for Dave Martinez. RF Paul O'Neill (.256) nearly doubled his previous top home-run output (16 to 28). LF Billy Hatcher (.262) is adequate, and rookie Reggie Sanders is ready to go in center. Joe Oliver (.216) and Jeff Reed (.267) will split the catching chores, at least until Dan Wilson is ready. Offensive shocker: The fifth-place '91 Reds hit 164 homers, 39 more than in their championship season.

So how did this club lose? You simply can't win without pitching, which is exactly what the Reds tried to do last season. The bullpen is good and capable of being better, led by closers Norm Charlton (3–5) and Rob Dibble (3–5, 31 saves). But beyond staff ace Jose Rijo (15–6, 2.51, Cy Young numbers), the rest of the group took '91 off. Cleveland's ace, Greg Swindell (9–16, 3.48, for a 57–105 club), and ex-Dodger Tim Belcher join the Cincy rotation, though the price was steep.

STAT LEADERS — 1991

BATTING
Average: Morris, .318
Runs: Sabo, 91
Hits: Sabo, 175
Doubles: O'Neill, 36
Triples: Duncan, Larkin, 4
Home runs: O'Neill, 28
RBIs: O'Neill, 91
Stolen bases: Larkin, 24

PITCHING
Wins: Rijo, 15
Losses: Browning, 14
Complete games: Rijo, 3
Shutouts: Rijo, 1
Saves: Dibble, 31
Walks: Myers, 80
Strikeouts: Rijo, 172

NL West
ATLANTA BRAVES
1991 Finish: First
1992 Prediction: Second

David Justice

Steve Avery

Forget about those long-suffering Atlanta
Braves fans. If they were suffering for all the
years their team lounged at the bottom of
the NL East, they weren't doing it at the
ballpark. But now that they've found their
way to Fulton County Stadium, this ball
club has the talent to keep them around.

Start with the fine young pitching, led by
lefties Tom Glavine (20–11, 2.55) and Steve
Avery (18–8, 3.38, after a 3–11 1990 season)
and right-hander John Smoltz (14–13, 3.80).
Add veteran LH Charlie Leibrandt (15–13),
and manager Bobby Cox can sleep easily
most nights. If '91 rookie Mark Wohlers
(3–1, 3.20) can do it for a full season, the
bullpen will be plenty strong, even if Juan
Berenguer and Alejandro Pena aren't back.

The club isn't without weaknesses. The

middle infield (SS Rafael Belliard, 2Bs Jeff Treadway and Mark Lemke) isn't up to the standards of the rest of the crowd. But MVP 3B Terry Pendleton (league-leading .319, 34 doubles, 86 RBIs) is the NL's best at third, and young Brian Hunter (.251) may be ready to blossom at 1B.

RF David Justice (.275, 87 RBIs, 21 HRs in only 109 games) should become a superstar any day now. But the best news is that the Braves won for the two months he was disabled last summer. CF Ronnie Gant (.251, 105 RBIs, 32 homers) is one of baseball's great success stories, bouncing back from the low minors in 1989. Otis Nixon (drug suspension) is back, so LF is set. Keith Mitchell (.318 in 48 games) provides plenty of depth here.

Ex-Cub C Damon Berryhill will have a shot at a starting role in '92, with Greg Olson still available. Summers should be fun in Atlanta for a long while.

STAT LEADERS — 1991

BATTING
Average: Pendleton, .319*
Runs: Gant, 101
Hits: Pendleton, 187*
Doubles: Gant, 35
Triples: Pendleton, 8
Home runs: Gant, 32
RBIs: Gant, 105
Stolen bases: Nixon, 72

*Led league.
**Tied for league lead.

PITCHING
Wins: Glavine, 20**
Losses: Leibrandt,
   Smoltz, 13
Complete games:
   Glavine, 9**
Shutouts: Three with 1
Saves: Berenguer, 17
Walks: Smoltz, 77
Strikeouts: Glavine, 192

NL West
LOS ANGELES DODGERS
1991 Finish: Second
1992 Prediction: Third

Brett Butler   **Ramon Martinez**

Though the Dodgers missed the '91 NL
West title by only one game (despite going
20–8 in September), the ball club finds itself
at the crossroads. There's lots of young talent in the L.A. organization. The question
is: Has their time finally come?

Probably not. There's no need for mas-
sive rebuilding (depending on how GM Fred
Claire fared in the free-agent wars). And
with manager Tom Lasorda winding down
his career (could '92 be his last year?), the
Dodgers will make an all-out effort to win
for Mr. Ultra Slim•Fast this season.

There are some sure shots, to be sure. CF
Brett Butler (.296, 38 steals), one of the top
free-agent pickups ever, plays next to RF
Darryl Strawberry (.265, 99 RBIs, 28 homers,
after a horrible start). Could rookie Tom

Goodwin become the LF? Probably not, with ex-Red (and Strawberry pal) Eric Davis on hand. After 1B Eddie Murray (.260, 96 RBIs) moved to the Mets, L.A. shipped OF Chris Gwynn to K.C. for Todd Benzinger. He'll hold the fort until Eric Karros is ready.

Barring any sudden changes, Jose Offerman (.195) should open the season at SS (he'll have to hit), with Lenny Harris (.287) and Mike Sharperson (.278) sharing time at second. Dave Hansen (.268) may rate a slight edge over Jeff Hamilton (.223) at third. Famed plate-blocker C Mike Scioscia (.264) may get help from rookie Carlos Hernandez.

With Orel Hershiser (7–2) re-signed and Bob Ojeda (12–9) a real possibility, Dodger pitching will rival Atlanta's. Ramon Martinez (17–13) leads the pack, which features ex-Blue Jay Tom Candiotti (13–13, 2.65) and Kevin Gross (10–11, mostly out of the bullpen). L.A. waits for Ramon's brother, Pedro Martinez (18–8, a nifty 2.28 in the minors in '91). The bullpen should hold up well.

STAT LEADERS — 1991

BATTING
Average: Butler, .296
Runs: Butler, 112*
Hits: Butler, 182
Doubles: Murray, 23
Triples: Samuel, 6
Home runs: Strawberry, 28
RBIs: Strawberry, 99
Stolen bases: Butler, 38

PITCHING
Wins: Martinez, 17
Losses: Martinez, 13
Complete games:
   Martinez, 6
Shutouts: Martinez, 4
Saves: Howell, 16
Walks: Belcher, 75
Strikeouts: Belcher, 156

*Led league.

NL West
SAN DIEGO PADRES
1991 Finish: Third
1992 Prediction: Fourth

Fred McGriff   **Tony Gwynn**

If the San Diego Padres can spend a little more time with manager Greg Riddoch
this season instead of with the team doc-
tor, the Padres can contend in the NL West
— and save Riddoch's job in the process.
Injuries to important folks like RF Tony
Gwynn, moody SS Tony Fernandez, and
pitchers Greg Harris and Ed Whitson left
San Diego 10 games behind the champion
Braves.

It will take more than good health, of
course. Lefty Bruce Hurst (15–8, 3.29) is the
ace of the mound staff, with major help from
right-handers Greg Harris (9–5, 2.23) and
Andy Benes (15–11, 3.03). After that, Riddoch has been forced to scramble. Righty
Ricky Bones should win a spot in '92. The
bullpen may show improvement. For open-

ers, closer Craig Lefferts (1–6, 23 saves) gets a partner in ex-Red Randy Myers.

1B Fred McGriff (.278, 31 homers, 106 RBIs) proved that he was everything the Padres hoped he'd be in his first NL season. Now that he knows the league, he should get even better, especially if San Diego can find another powerman to prevent opponents from pitching around him. With Bip Roberts off to Cincy for relief ace Myers, there may be a scramble at 2B. Like the girl with the curl in the nursery rhyme, SS Fernandez (.272) can be very good (when he's good), not so hot when he's not. Barring a deal, 3B is a problem.

RF Gwynn (.317) just missed another NL bat title and remains one of the game's most beautiful hitters. Darrin Jackson (.262, 21 homers) was last year's most pleasant surprise. Catching is in superior shape as long as Benito Santiago (.267, 87 RBIs) is around. But almost every San Diego trade discussion mentions the talented backstop.

STAT LEADERS — 1991

BATTING
Average: Gwynn, .317
Runs: McGriff, 84
Hits: Gwynn, 168
Doubles: Fernandez, Gwynn, 27
Triples: Gwynn, 11
Home runs: McGriff, 31
RBIs: McGriff, 106
Stolen bases: Roberts, 26

PITCHING
Wins: Benes, Hurst, 15
Losses: Rasmussen, 13
Complete games: Benes, Hurst, 4
Shutouts: Harris, 2
Saves: Lefferts, 23
Walks: Benes, Hurst, 59
Strikeouts: Benes, 167

NL West
SAN FRANCISCO GIANTS
1991 Finish: Fourth
1992 Prediction: Fifth

Robby Thompson   **Matt Williams**

Pitching — actually the lack of it — wrecked the Giants' 1991 season, and unless president Al Rosen comes up with some soon, the '92 results could be even worse. There were lots of unhappy people at Candlestick Park last season, most of them wearing Giants uniforms.

Outside of the mound crew, the rest of the club is actually in decent shape. All-Pro 1B Will Clark (.301, 116 RBIs) hits — and fields — like a machine. If you're building a ball club, you could easily start with him. 2B Robby Thompson (.262, 19 homers) is solid on defense and shows decent power at the plate. SS Jose Uribe (.221) has played himself out of a job. So look for heralded rookie Royce Clayton (.280 at Shreveport) to take over. They don't get any better than 3B Matt

Williams (.268, 34 homers, 98 RBIs). But SF gave up on talented but troubled LF Kevin Mitchell (.256, 27 homers) to bring fresh arms (ex-Mariners Billy Swift [17 saves], Mike Jackson [14 saves], and Dave Burba) to Candlestick. The arms are ordinary; Mitchell is not. SF might look bad on this one!

The Giants will need more production from Willie McGee (.312) and Mike Felder (.264), especially if unhappy Kevin Bass is out of there. The Giants' catching is lousy. Kirt Manwaring can hit a little; neither he nor Steve Decker is much behind the bat.

The pitching stock rises considerably if '91 flop Bud Black (12–16, 25 homers served) bounces back. Otherwise, it's just John Burkett (12–11, 4.18) and Trevor Wilson (13–11, 3.56, after winning 9 of his last 11) and not much else. Dave Righetti (2–7, 24 saves) is one of the better closers.

Can the offense and defense carry the pitching? Possible, but unlikely.

STAT LEADERS — 1991

BATTING
Average: McGee, .312
Runs: Clark, 84
Hits: Clark, 170
Doubles: Clark, 32
Triples: Clark, 7
Home runs: Williams, 34
RBIs: Clark, 116
Stolen bases: Felder, 21

PITCHING
Wins: Wilson, 13
Losses: Black, 16*
Complete games: Black, Burkett, 3
Shutouts: Black, 3
Saves: Righetti, 24
Walks: Wilson, 77
Strikeouts: Wilson, 139

*Led league.

NL West
HOUSTON ASTROS
1991 Finish: Sixth
1992 Prediction: Sixth

Craig Biggio   **Jeff Bagwell**

If Houston Astro fans need a dream to latch on to, they need look only as far as Atlanta. This isn't to say that the 'Stros are ready to go from last to first in Braves fashion. Manager Art Howe suffered through a 65–97 season a year ago, grooming his ball club for a run in, let's say, 1994 or so. Patience, Houston fans.

The NL's top '91 rookie, 1B Jeff Bagwell (.294, 15 homers, 82 RBIs), is set for years to come. He'll probably be joined by future star SS Andujar Cedeno (.243) and 3B Ken Caminiti (.253). Second base is the trouble spot. If Scooter Tucker or ex-Indian Ed Taubensee can catch, Astro star C Craig Biggio (.295) could move to 2B.

The outfield will feature more youngsters, like leadoff hitter Steve Finley (.285).

Luis Gonzalez (.254) will be back, too, along with talented Eric Anthony, who gets one more (last?) chance in '92.

Right-hander Pete Harnisch (12–9, a sparkling 2.70) is the key to the young pitching staff that is overpowering one day, wild the next. Righties Jeff Juden and Brian Williams, who rose from Class A to the big club last season, should win full-time jobs in the rotation, along with young veteran Darryl Kile (he's only 23) and ex-Indian Willie Blair. They just need time. If Jimmy Jones (elbow surgery) manages to bounce back, so much the better.

The bullpen is a tougher call. Righty Mark Portugal may be tested as the team's closer, with last year's closer, lefty Al Osuna (7–6, 12 saves), as the set-up man. Right-hander Curt Schilling (3–5, 8 saves) still fits here.

A month-long road trip during the Republican National Convention at the Astrodome won't help any, but '92 is just a building year for this young club.

STAT LEADERS — 1991

BATTING
Average: Biggio, .295
Runs: Finley, 84
Hits: Finley, 170
Doubles: Caminiti, 30
Triples: Finley, 10
Home runs: Bagwell, 15
RBIs: Bagwell, 82
Stolen bases: Finley, 34

PITCHING
Wins: Harnisch, 12
Losses: Deshaies,
  Portugal, 12
Complete games:
  Harnisch, 4
Shutouts: Harnisch, 2
Saves: Osuna, 12
Walks: Kile, 84
Strikeouts: Harnisch, 172

The defending NL homer and RBI king, Met star Howard Johnson, starts a new adventure by moving to right field at Shea in '92.

1991
STATISTICS

AMERICAN LEAGUE
Batting

(32 or more at-bats)
*Bats Left-Handed †Switch-Hitter

Batter and Team	AVG	G	AB	R	H	HR	RBI	SB
Abner, S., Cal.	.228	41	101	12	23	2	9	1
Aldrete, M., Cle.*	.262	85	183	22	48	1	19	1
Allanson, A., Det.	.232	60	151	10	35	1	16	0
Allred, B., Cle.*	.232	48	125	17	29	3	12	2
Alomar, R., Tor.†	.295	161	637	88	188	9	69	53
Alomar, S., Cle.	.217	51	184	10	40	0	7	0
Anderson, B., Bal.*	.230	113	256	40	59	2	27	12
Baerga, C., Cle.†	.288	158	593	80	171	11	69	3
Baines, H., Oak.*	.295	141	488	76	144	20	90	0
Barfield, J., N.Y.	.225	84	284	37	64	17	48	1
Barnes, S., Det.	.289	75	159	28	46	5	17	10
Bell, J., Bal.†	.172	100	209	26	36	1	15	0
Belle, A., Cle.	.282	123	461	60	130	28	95	3
Benzinger, T., K.C.†	.294	78	293	29	86	2	40	2
Bergman, D., Det.	.237	86	194	23	46	7	29	1
Berry. S., K.C.	.133	31	60	5	8	0	1	0
Bichette, D., Mil.	.238	134	445	53	106	15	59	14
Blankenship, L., Oak.	.249	90	185	33	46	3	21	12
Blowers, M., N.Y.	.200	15	35	3	7	1	1	0
Boggs, W., Bos.*	.332	144	546	93	181	8	51	1
Borders, P., Tor.	.244	105	291	22	71	5	36	0
Bordick, M., Oak.	.238	90	235	21	56	0	21	3
Bradley, S., Sea.*	.203	83	172	10	35	0	11	0
Brett, G., K.C.*	.255	131	505	77	129	10	61	2
Briley, G., Sea.*	.260	139	381	39	99	2	26	23
Brock, G., Mil.*	.283	31	60	9	17	1	6	1
Broisus, S., Oak.	.235	36	68	9	16	2	4	3
Brown, J., Min.	.216	38	37	10	8	0	0	7
Browne, J., Cle.†	.228	107	290	28	66	1	29	2

Batter and Team	AVG	G	AB	R	H	HR	RBI	SB
Brumley, M., Bos.†	.212	63	118	16	25	0	5	2
Brunansky, T., Bos.	.229	142	459	54	105	16	70	1
Buechele, S., Tex.	.267	121	416	58	111	18	66	0
Buhner, J., Sea.	.244	137	406	64	99	27	77	0
Burks, E., Bos.	.251	130	474	56	119	14	56	6
Bush, R., Min.*	.303	93	165	21	50	6	23	0
Canale, G., Mil.*	.176	21	34	6	6	3	10	0
Canseco, J., Oak.	.266	154	572	115	152	44	122	26
Carter, J., Tor.	.273	162	638	89	174	33	108	20
Clark, J., Bos.	.249	140	481	75	120	28	87	0
Cochrane, D., Sea.†	.247	65	178	16	44	2	22	0
Cole, A., Cle.*	.295	122	387	58	114	0	21	27
Cooper, S., Bos.*	.457	14	35	6	16	0	7	0
Cora, J., Chi.†	.241	100	228	37	55	0	18	11
Cotto, H., Sea.	.305	66	177	35	54	6	23	16
Cromartie, W., K.C.*	.313	69	131	13	41	1	20	1
Cuyler, M., Det.†	.257	154	475	77	122	3	33	41
Daugherty, J., Tex.†	.194	58	144	8	28	1	11	1
Davis, A., Sea.*	.221	145	462	39	102	12	69	0
Davis, C., Min.†	.277	153	534	84	148	29	93	5
Davis, G., Bal.	.227	49	176	29	40	10	28	4
Deer, R., Det.	.179	134	448	64	80	25	64	1
Dempsey, R., Mil.	.231	61	147	15	34	4	21	0
Devereaux, M., Bal.	.260	149	608	82	158	19	59	16
Diaz, M., Tex.	.264	96	182	24	48	1	22	0
Disarcina, G., Cal.	.211	18	57	5	12	0	3	0
Downing, B., Tex.	.278	123	407	76	113	17	49	1
Ducey, R., Tor.*	.235	39	68	8	16	1	4	2
Eisenreich J., K.C.*	.301	135	375	47	113	2	47	5
Espinoza, A., N.Y.	.256	148	480	51	123	5	33	4
Evans, D., Bal.	.270	101	270	35	73	6	38	2
Felix, J., Cal.†	.283	66	230	32	65	2	26	7
Fermin, F., Cle.	.262	129	424	30	111	0	31	5
Fielder, C., Det.	.261	162	624	102	163	44	133	0
Fisk, C., Chi.	.241	134	460	42	111	18	74	1
Fletcher, S., Chi.	.206	90	248	14	51	1	28	0
Franco, J., Tex.	.341	146	589	108	201	15	78	36

Batter and Team	AVG	G	AB	R	H	HR	RBI	SB
Fryman, T., Det.	.259	149	557	65	144	21	91	12
Gaetti, G., Cal.	.246	152	586	58	144	18	66	5
Gagne, G., Min.	.265	139	408	52	108	8	42	11
Gallagher, D., Cal.	.293	90	270	32	79	1	30	2
Gallego, M., Oak.	.247	159	482	67	119	12	49	6
Gantner, J., Mil.*	.283	140	526	63	149	2	47	4
Geren, R., N.Y.	.219	64	128	7	28	2	12	0
Gibson, K., K.C.*	.236	132	462	81	109	16	55	18
Gladden, D., Min.	.247	126	461	65	114	6	52	15
Gomez, L., Bal.	.233	118	391	40	91	16	45	1
Gonzales, R., Tor.	.195	71	118	16	23	1	6	0
Gonzales, J., Cle.	.159	33	69	10	11	1	4	8
Gonzalez, J., Tex.	.264	142	545	78	144	27	102	4
Grebeck, C., Chi.	.281	107	224	37	63	6	31	1
Greenwell, M., Bos.*	.300	147	544	76	163	9	83	15
Griffey, Jr., K., Sea.*	.327	154	548	76	179	22	100	18
Griffey, Sr., K., Sea.*	.282	30	85	10	24	1	9	0
Gruber, K., Tor.	.252	113	429	58	108	20	65	12
Guillen, O., Chi.*	.273	154	524	52	143	3	49	21
Hall, M., N.Y.*	.285	141	492	67	140	19	80	0
Hamilton, D., Mil.*	.311	122	405	64	126	1	57	16
Harper, B., Min.	.311	123	441	54	137	10	69	1
Henderson, D., Oak.	.276	150	572	86	158	25	85	6
Henderson, R., Oak.	.268	134	470	105	126	18	57	58
Hernandez, J., Tex.	.184	45	98	8	18	0	4	0
Hill, D., Cal.†	.239	77	209	36	50	1	20	1
Hill, G., Tor.-Cle.	.258	72	221	29	57	8	25	6
Hoiles, C., Bal.	.243	107	341	36	83	11	31	0
Horn, S., Bal.*	.233	121	317	45	74	23	61	0
Howard, D., K.C.†	.216	94	236	20	51	1	17	3
Howell, J., Cal.*	.210	32	81	11	17	2	7	1
Howitt, D., Oak.*	.167	21	42	5	7	1	3	0
Hrbek, K., Min.*	.284	132	462	72	131	20	89	4
Huff, M., Cle.-Chi.	.251	102	243	42	61	3	25	14
Hulett, T., Bal.	.204	79	206	29	42	7	18	0
Humphreys, M., N.Y.	.200	25	40	9	8	0	3	2
Huson, J., Tex.*	.213	119	268	36	57	2	26	8

Batter and Team	AVG	G	AB	R	H	HR	RBI	SB
Incaviglia, P., Det.	.214	97	337	38	72	11	38	1
Jackson, B., Chi.	.225	23	71	8	16	3	14	0
Jacoby, B., Cle.-Oak.	.224	122	419	28	94	4	14	2
James, C., Cle.	.238	115	437	31	104	5	41	3
Jefferson, R., Cle.†	.198	26	101	10	20	2	12	0
Johnson, L., Chi.*	.274	159	588	72	161	0	49	26
Jones, T., Sea.	.251	79	175	30	44	3	24	2
Joyner, W., Cal.*	.301	143	551	79	166	21	96	2
Karkovice, R., Chi.	.246	75	167	25	41	5	22	0
Kelly, P., N.Y.	.242	96	298	35	72	3	23	12
Kelly, R., N.Y.	.267	126	486	68	130	20	69	32
Kirby, W., Cle.*	.209	21	43	4	9	0	5	1
Kittle, R., Chi.	.191	17	47	7	9	2	7	0
Knoblauch, C., Min.	.281	151	565	78	159	1	50	25
Larkin, G., Min.†	.286	98	255	34	73	2	19	2
Law, V., Oak.	.209	74	134	11	28	0	9	0
Lee, M., Tor.†	.234	138	445	41	104	0	29	7
Leius, S., Min.	.286	109	199	35	57	5	20	5
Lewis, M., Cle.	.264	84	314	29	83	0	30	2
Leyritz, J., N.Y.	.182	32	77	8	14	0	4	0
Livingston, S., Det.*	.291	44	127	19	37	2	11	2
Lopez, L., Cle.	.220	35	82	7	18	0	7	0
Lovullo, T., N.Y.†	.176	22	51	0	9	0	2	0
Lyons, S., Bos.*	.241	87	212	15	51	4	17	10
Maas, K., N.Y.*	.220	148	500	69	110	23	63	5
Macfarlane, M., K.C.	.277	84	267	34	74	13	41	1
Mack, S., Min.	.310	143	442	79	137	18	74	13
Maldonado, C., Mil.-Tor. ...	.250	86	288	37	72	12	48	4
Manto, J., Cle.	.211	47	128	15	27	2	13	2
Marshall, M., Bos.-Cal.	.261	24	69	4	18	1	7	0
Martinez, C., K.C.	.207	44	121	17	25	4	17	0
Martinez, C., Bal.*	.269	67	216	32	58	13	33	1
Martinez, C. Cle.	.284	72	257	22	73	5	30	3
Martinez, E., Sea.	.307	150	544	98	167	14	52	0
Martinez, T., Sea.*	.205	36	112	11	23	4	9	0
Marzano, J., Bos.	.263	49	114	10	30	0	9	0
Mattingly, D., N.Y.*	.288	152	587	64	169	9	68	2

Batter and Team	AVG	G	AB	R	H	HR	RBI	SB
Mayne, B., K.C.*	.251	85	231	22	58	3	31	2
McGwire, M., Oak.	.201	154	483	62	97	22	75	2
McKnight, J., Bal.†	.171	16	41	2	7	0	2	1
McRae, B., K.C.†	.261	152	629	86	164	8	64	20
Melvin, B., Bal.	.250	79	228	11	57	1	23	0
Mercedes, L., Bal.	.204	19	54	10	11	0	2	0
Merullo, M., Chi.*	.229	80	140	8	32	5	21	0
Meulens, H., N.Y.	.222	96	288	37	64	6	29	3
Milligan, R., Bal.	.263	141	483	57	127	16	70	0
Molitor, P., Mil.	.325	158	665	133	216	17	75	19
Moseby, L., Det.*	.262	74	260	37	68	6	35	8
Mulliniks, R., Tor.*	.250	97	240	27	60	2	24	0
Munoz, P., Min.	.283	51	138	15	39	7	26	3
Myers, G. Tor.*	.262	107	309	25	81	8	36	0
Naehring, T., Bos.	.109	20	55	1	6	0	3	0
Newman, A., Min.†	.191	118	246	25	47	0	19	4
Newson, W., Chi.*	.295	71	132	20	39	4	25	2
Nokes, M., N.Y.*	.268	135	456	52	122	24	77	3
O'Brien, P., Sea.*	.248	152	560	58	139	17	88	0
Olerud, J., Tor.*	.256	139	454	64	116	17	68	0
Orsulak, J., Bal.*	.278	143	486	57	135	5	43	6
Ortiz, J., Min.	.209	61	134	9	28	0	11	0
Orton, J., Cal.	.203	29	69	7	14	0	3	0
Pagliarulo, M., Min.*	.279	121	365	38	102	6	36	1
Palmeiro, R., Tex.*	.322	159	631	115	203	26	88	4
Palmer, D., Tex.	.187	81	268	38	50	15	37	0
Parker, D., Cal.-Tor.*	.239	132	502	47	120	11	59	3
Parrish, L., Cal.	.216	119	402	38	87	19	51	0
Pasqua, D., Chi.*	.259	134	417	71	108	18	66	0
Pecota, B., K.C.	.286	125	398	53	114	6	45	16
Pena, T., Bos.	.231	141	464	45	107	5	48	8
Petralli, G., Tex.*	.271	87	199	21	54	2	20	2
Pettis, G., Tex.†	.216	137	282	37	61	0	19	29
Phillips, T., Det.†	.284	146	564	87	160	17	72	10
Plantier, P., Bos.*	.331	53	148	27	49	11	35	1
Polonia, L., Cal.*	.296	150	604	92	179	2	50	48
Powell, A., Sea.	.216	57	111	16	24	3	12	0

Batter and Team	AVG	G	AB	R	H	HR	RBI	SB
Puckett, K., Min.	.319	152	611	92	195	15	89	11
Pulliam, H., K.C.	.273	18	33	4	9	3	4	0
Quintana, C., Bos.	.295	149	478	69	141	11	71	1
Quirk, J., Oak.*	.261	76	203	16	53	1	17	0
Raines, T., Chi.†	.268	155	609	102	163	5	50	51
Randolph, W., Mil.	.327	124	431	60	141	0	54	4
Reed, J., Bos.	.283	153	618	87	175	5	60	6
Reimer, K., Tex.*	.269	136	394	46	106	20	69	0
Reynolds, H., Sea.†	.254	161	631	95	160	3	57	28
Riles, E., Oak.*	.214	108	281	30	60	5	32	3
Ripken, B., Bal.	.216	104	287	24	62	0	14	0
Ripken, C., Bal.	.323	162	650	99	210	34	114	6
Rivera, L., Bos.	.258	129	414	64	107	8	40	4
Rodriguez, C., N.Y.†	.189	15	37	1	7	0	2	0
Rodriguez, I., Tex.	.264	88	280	24	74	3	27	0
Romine, K., Bos.	.164	44	55	7	9	1	7	1
Rose, B., Cal.	.277	22	65	5	18	1	8	0
Salas, M., Det.*	.088	33	57	2	5	1	7	0
Sax, S., N.Y.	.304	158	652	85	198	10	56	31
Schaefer, J., Sea.	.250	84	164	19	41	1	11	3
Schofield, D., Cal.	.225	134	427	44	96	0	31	8
Segui, D., Bal.†	.278	86	212	15	59	2	22	1
Seitzer, K., K.C.	.265	85	234	28	62	1	25	4
Sheffield, G., Mil.	.194	50	175	25	34	2	22	5
Shelby, J., Det.†	.154	53	143	19	22	3	8	0
Sheridan, P., N.Y.*	.204	62	113	13	23	4	7	1
Shumpert, T., K.C.	.217	144	369	45	80	5	34	17
Sierra, R., Tex.†	.307	161	661	110	203	25	116	16
Skinner, J., Cle.	.243	99	284	23	69	1	24	0
Snyder, C., Chi.-Tor.	.175	71	166	14	29	3	17	0
Sojo, L., Cal.	.258	113	364	38	94	3	20	4
Sorrento, P., Min.*	.255	26	47	6	12	4	13	0
Sosa, S., Chi.	.203	116	316	39	64	10	33	13
Spehr, T., K.C.	.189	37	74	7	14	3	14	1
Spiers, B., Mil.*	.283	133	414	71	117	8	54	14
Sprague, E., Tor.	.275	61	160	17	44	4	20	0
Stanley, M., Tex.	.249	95	181	25	45	3	25	0

Batter and Team	AVG	G	AB	R	H	HR	RBI	SB
Steinbach, T., Oak.	.274	129	456	50	125	6	67	2
Stevens, L., Cal.*	.293	18	58	8	17	0	9	1
Stillwell, K., K.C.†	.265	122	385	44	102	6	51	3
Stubbs, F., Mil.*	.213	103	362	48	77	11	38	13
Surhoff, B., Mil.*	.289	143	505	57	146	5	68	5
Sveum, D., Mil.†	.241	90	266	33	64	4	43	2
Tabler, P., Tor.	.216	82	185	20	40	1	21	0
Tartabull, D., K.C.	.316	132	484	78	153	31	100	6
Taubensee, E., Cle.*	.242	26	66	5	16	0	8	0
Tettleton, M., Det.†	.263	154	501	85	132	31	89	3
Thomas, F., Chi.	.318	158	559	104	178	32	109	1
Thome, J., Cle.*	.255	27	98	7	25	1	9	1
Thurman, G., K.C.	.277	80	184	24	51	2	13	15
Tingley, R., Cal.	.200	45	115	11	23	1	13	1
Trammell, A., Det.	.248	101	375	57	93	9	55	11
Valle, D., Sea.	.194	132	324	38	63	8	32	0
Vaughn, G., Mil.	.244	145	542	81	132	27	98	2
Vaughn, M., Bos.*	.260	74	219	21	57	4	32	2
Velarde, R., N.Y.	.245	80	184	19	45	1	15	3
Venable, M., Cal.*	.246	82	187	24	46	3	21	2
Ventura, R., Chi.*	.284	157	606	92	172	23	100	2
Vizquel, O., Sea.†	.230	142	426	42	98	1	41	7
Walling, D., Tex.*	.091	24	44	1	4	0	2	0
Ward, T., Cle.-Tor.†	.239	48	113	12	27	0	7	0
Webster, L., Min.	.294	18	34	7	10	3	8	0
Webster, M., Cle.†	.125	13	32	2	4	0	0	2
Weiss, W., Oak.†	.226	40	133	15	30	0	13	6
Whitaker, L., Det.*	.279	138	470	94	131	23	78	4
White, D., Tor.†	.282	156	642	110	181	17	60	33
Whiten, M., Tor.-Cle.†	.243	116	407	46	99	9	45	4
Whitt, E., Bal.*	.242	35	62	5	15	0	3	0
Williams, B., N.Y.†	.238	85	320	43	76	3	34	10
Wilson, M., Tor.†	.241	86	241	26	58	2	28	11
Wilson, W., Oak.†	.238	113	294	38	70	0	28	20
Winfield, D., Cal.	.262	150	568	75	149	28	86	7
Worthington, C., Bal.	.225	31	102	11	23	4	12	0
Yount, R., Mil.	.260	130	503	66	131	10	77	6

AMERICAN LEAGUE
Pitching
(78 or more innings pitched)
*Throws Left-Handed

Pitcher and Team	W	L	ERA	G	IP	H	BB	SO
Abbott, J., Cal.*	18	11	2.89	34	243.0	222	73	158
Acker, J., Tor.	3	5	5.20	54	88.1	77	36	44
Alexander, G., Tex.	5	3	5.24	30	89.1	93	48	50
Anderson, A., Min.*	5	11	4.96	29	134.1	148	42	51
Appier, K., K.C.	13	10	3.42	34	207.2	205	61	158
Aquino, L., K.C.	8	4	3.44	38	157.0	152	47	80
August, D., Mil.	9	8	5.47	28	138.1	166	47	62
Ballard, J., Bal.*	6	12	5.60	26	123.2	153	28	37
Barfield, J., Tex.*	4	4	4.54	28	83.1	96	22	27
Boddicker, M., K.C.	12	12	4.08	30	180.2	188	59	79
Bolton, T., Bos.*	8	9	5.24	25	110.0	136	51	64
Bosio, C., Mil.	14	10	3.25	32	204.2	187	58	117
Brown, K., Tex.	9	12	4.40	33	210.2	233	90	96
Cadaret, G., N.Y.*	8	6	3.62	68	121.2	110	59	105
Candiotti, T., Cle.-Tor.	13	13	2.65	34	238.0	202	73	167
Cerutti, J., Det.*	3	6	4.57	38	88.2	94	37	29
Clemens, R., Bos.	18	10	2.62	35	271.1	219	65	241
Crim, C., Mil.	8	5	4.63	66	91.1	115	25	39
Davis, S., K.C.	3	9	4.96	51	114.1	140	46	53
DeLucia, R., Sea.	12	13	5.09	32	182.0	176	78	98
Eichhorn, M., Cal.	3	3	1.98	70	81.2	63	13	49
Erickson, S., Min.	20	8	3.18	32	204.0	189	7	108
Fernandez, A., Chi.	9	13	4.51	34	191.2	186	88	145
Finley, C., Cal.*	18	9	3.80	34	227.1	205	101	171
Flanagan, M., Bal.*	2	7	2.38	64	98.1	84	25	55
Frohwirth, T., Bal.	7	3	1.87	51	96.1	64	29	77
Garcia, R., Chi.	4	4	5.40	16	78.1	79	31	40
Gardiner, M., Bos.	9	10	4.85	22	130.0	140	47	91
Gibson, P., Det.*	5	7	4.59	68	96.0	112	48	52

Pitcher and Team	W	L	ERA	G	IP	H	BB	SO
Gordon, T., K.C.	9	14	3.87	45	158.0	129	87	167
Gubicza, M., K.C.	9	12	5.68	26	133.0	168	42	89
Guetterman, L., N.Y.*	3	4	3.68	64	88.0	91	25	35
Gullickson, B., Det. 20		9	3.90	35	226.1	256	44	91
Guthrie, M., Min.*	7	5	4.32	41	98.0	116	41	72
Guzman, J., Tex. 13		7	3.08	25	169.2	152	84	125
Guzman, J., Tor. 10		3	2.99	23	138.2	98	66	123
Habyan, J., N.Y.	4	2	2.30	66	90.0	73	20	70
Hanson, E., Sea.	8	8	3.81	27	174.2	182	56	143
Harris, G., Bos. 11		12	3.85	53	173.0	157	69	127
Harvey, B., Cal.	2	4	1.60	67	78.2	51	17	101
Hawkins, A., N.Y.-Oak. ...	4	6	5.52	19	89.2	91	42	45
Henneman, M., Det. 10		2	2.88	60	84.1	81	34	61
Hesketh, J., Bos.* 12		4	3.29	39	153.1	142	53	104
Hibbard, G., Chi.* 11		11	4.31	32	194.0	196	57	71
Hillegas, S., Cle.	3	4	4.34	51	83.0	67	46	66
Holman, B., Sea. 13		14	3.69	30	195.1	199	77	108
Hough, C., Chi.	9	10	4.02	31	199.1	167	94	107
Jackson, M., Sea.	7	7	3.25	72	88.2	64	34	74
Jeffcoat, M., Tex.*	5	3	4.63	70	79.2	104	25	43
Johnson, D., Bal.	4	8	7.07	22	84.0	127	24	38
Johnson J., N.Y.*	6	11	5.95	23	127.0	156	33	62
Johnson, R., Sea.* 13		10	3.98	33	201.1	151	152	228
Key, J., Tor.* 16		12	3.05	33	209.1	207	44	125
King, E., Cle.	6	11	4.60	25	150.2	166	44	59
Krueger, B., Sea.* 11		8	3.60	35	175.0	194	60	91
Lamp, D., Bos.	6	3	4.70	51	92.0	100	31	57
Langston, M., Cal.* 19		8	3.00	34	246.1	190	96	183
Leary, T., N.Y.	4	10	6.49	28	120.2	150	57	83
Leiter, M., Det.	9	7	4.21	38	134.2	125	50	103
Machado, J., Mil.	3	3	3.45	54	88.2	65	55	98
McCaskill, K., Cal. 10		19	4.26	30	177.2	193	66	71
McDonald, B., Bal.	6	8	4.84	21	126.1	126	43	85
McDowell, J., Chi. 17		10	3.41	35	253.2	212	82	191
Mesa, J., Bal.	6	11	5.97	23	123.2	151	62	64
Milacki, B., Bal. 10		9	4.01	31	184.0	175	53	108
Montgomery, J., K.C.	4	4	2.90	67	90.0	83	28	77

Pitcher and Team	W	L	ERA	G	IP	H	BB	SO
Moore, M., Oak.	17	8	2.96	33	210.0	176	105	153
Morris, J., Min.	18	12	3.43	35	246.2	226	92	163
Morton, K., Bos.*	6	5	4.59	16	86.1	93	40	45
Mussina, M., Bal.	4	5	2.87	12	87.2	77	21	52
Nagy, C., Cle.	10	15	4.13	33	211.1	228	66	109
Navarro, J., Mil.	15	12	3.92	34	234.0	237	73	114
Nichols, R., Cle.	2	11	3.54	31	137.1	145	30	76
Otto, D., Cle.*	2	8	4.23	18	100.0	108	27	47
Perez, M., Chi.	8	7	3.12	49	135.2	111	52	128
Plesac, D., Mil.*	2	7	4.29	45	92.1	92	39	61
Plunk, E., N.Y.	2	5	4.76	43	111.2	128	62	103
Robinson, J., Bal.	4	9	5.18	21	104.1	119	51	65
Rogers, K., Tex.*	10	10	5.42	63	109.2	121	61	73
Russell, J., Tex.	6	4	3.29	68	79.1	71	26	52
Ryan, N., Tex.	12	6	2.91	27	173.0	102	72	203
Saberhagen, B., K.C.	13	8	3.07	28	196.1	165	45	136
Sanderson, S., N.Y.	16	10	3.81	34	208.0	200	29	130
Slusarski, J., Oak.	5	7	5.27	20	109.1	121	52	60
Smith, R., Bal.	5	4	5.60	17	80.1	99	24	25
Stewart, D., Oak.	11	11	5.18	35	226.0	245	105	144
Stottlemyre, T., Tor.	15	8	3.78	34	219.0	194	75	116
Swan, R., Sea.*	6	2	3.43	63	78.2	81	28	33
Swift, B., Sea.	1	2	1.99	71	90.1	74	26	48
Swindell, G., Cle.*	9	16	3.48	33	238.0	241	31	169
Tanana, F., Det.*	13	12	3.77	33	217.1	217	78	107
Tapani, K., Min.	16	9	2.99	34	244.0	225	40	135
Taylor, W., N.Y.	7	12	6.27	23	116.1	144	53	72
Terrell, W., Det.	12	14	4.24	35	218.2	257	79	80
Timlin, M., Tor.	11	6	3.16	63	108.1	94	50	85
Ward, D., Tor.	7	6	2.77	81	107.1	80	33	132
Wegman, B., Mil.	15	7	2.84	28	193.1	176	40	89
Welch, B., Oak.	12	13	4.58	35	220.0	220	91	101
Wells, D., Tor.*	15	10	3.72	40	198.1	188	49	106
Williamson, M., Bal.	5	5	4.48	65	80.1	87	35	53
Willis, C., Min.	8	3	2.63	40	89.0	76	19	53
Witt, B., Tex.	3	7	6.09	17	88.2	84	74	82
Young, M., Bos*	3	7	5.18	19	88.2	92	53	69

NATIONAL LEAGUE
Batting

(42 or more at-bats)
*Bats Left-Handed   †Switch-Hitter

Batter and Team	AVG	G	AB	R	H	HR	RBI	SB
Abner, S., S.D.	.165	53	115	15	19	1	5	0
Alicea, I., St.L.†	.191	56	68	5	13	0	0	0
Anderson, D., S.F.	.248	100	226	24	56	2	13	2
Anthony, E., Hou.*	.153	39	118	11	18	1	7	1
Avery, S., Atl.*	.215	37	79	4	17	0	2	1
Azocar, O., S.D.*	.246	38	57	5	14	0	9	2
Backman, W., Phi.†	.243	94	185	20	45	0	15	3
Bagwell, J., Hou.	.294	156	554	79	163	15	82	7
Barberie, B., Mon.	.353	57	136	16	48	2	18	0
Barnes, B., Mon.*	.082	28	49	1	4	0	1	0
Bass, K., S.F.†	.233	124	361	43	84	10	40	7
Belcher, T., L.A.	.119	33	67	3	8	0	3	0
Bell, G., Chi.	.285	149	558	63	159	25	86	2
Bell, J., Pit.	.270	157	608	96	164	16	67	10
Belliard, R., Atl.	.249	149	353	36	88	0	27	3
Benavides, Cin.	.286	24	63	11	18	0	3	1
Benes, A., S.D.	.032	33	62	4	2	1	1	0
Benjamin, M., S.F.	.123	54	106	12	13	2	8	3
Benzinger, T., Cin.†	.187	51	123	7	23	1	11	2
Berryhill, D., Chi.-Atl.†	.188	63	160	13	30	5	14	1
Bielecki, M., Chi.-Atl.	.065	41	46	1	3	0	7	0
Biggio, C., Hou.	.295	149	546	79	161	4	46	19
Black, B., S.F.*	.183	35	71	3	13	0	6	0
Blauser, J., Atl.	.259	129	352	49	91	11	54	5
Bonds, B., Pit.*	.292	153	510	95	149	25	116	43
Bonilla, B., Pit.†	.302	157	577	102	174	18	100	2
Booker, R., Phi.*	.226	28	53	3	12	0	7	0

Batter and Team	AVG	G	AB	R	H	HR	RBI	SB
Boston, D., N.Y.*	.275	137	255	40	70	4	21	15
Braggs, G., Cin.	.260	85	250	36	65	11	39	11
Bream, S., Atl.*	.253	91	265	32	67	11	45	0
Brooks, H., N.Y.	.238	103	357	48	85	16	50	3
Browning, T., Cin.*	.171	36	70	3	12	1	5	0
Buechele, S., Pit.	.246	31	114	16	28	4	19	0
Bullock, E., Mon.*	.222	73	72	6	16	1	6	6
Burkett, J., S.F.	.091	36	55	0	5	0	1	0
Butler, B., L.A.*	.296	161	615	112	182	2	38	38
Cabrera, F., Atl.	.242	44	95	7	23	4	23	1
Calderon, I., Mon.	.300	134	470	69	141	19	75	31
Caminiti, K., Hou.†	.253	152	574	65	145	13	80	4
Candaele, C., Hou.†	.262	151	461	44	121	4	50	9
Carreon, M., N.Y.	.260	106	254	18	66	4	21	2
Carter, G., L.A.	.246	101	248	22	61	6	26	2
Castillo, B., Phi.	.173	28	52	3	9	0	2	1
Cedeno, A., Hou.	.243	67	251	27	61	9	36	4
Cerone, R., N.Y.	.273	90	227	18	62	2	16	1
Chamberlain, W., Phi.	.240	101	383	51	92	13	50	9
Clark, J., S.D.	.228	118	369	26	84	10	47	2
Clark, W., S.F.*	.301	148	565	84	170	29	116	4
Coleman, V., N.Y.†	.255	72	278	45	71	1	17	37
Cone, D., N.Y.*	.125	34	72	3	9	0	5	0
Coolbaugh, S., S.D.	.217	60	180	12	39	2	15	0
Daniels, K., L.A.*	.249	137	461	54	115	17	73	6
Dascenzo, D., Chi.†	.255	118	239	40	61	1	18	14
Daulton, D., Phi.*	.196	89	285	36	56	12	42	5
Davidson, M., Hou.	.190	85	142	10	27	2	15	0
Davis, E., Cin.	.235	89	285	39	67	11	33	14
Dawson, A., Chi.	.272	149	563	69	153	31	104	4
DeJesus, J., Phi.	.129	31	62	3	8	0	4	0
DeLeon, J., St.L.	.043	28	46	0	2	0	0	0
Decker, S., S.F.	.206	79	233	11	48	5	24	0
DeShields, D., Mon.*	.238	151	563	83	134	10	51	56
Donnels, C., N.Y.*	.225	37	89	7	20	0	5	1
Doran, B., Cin.†	.280	111	361	51	101	6	35	5
Drabek, D., Pit.	.179	36	84	6	15	0	2	0

Batter and Team	AVG	G	AB	R	H	HR	RBI	SB
Duncan, M., Cin.	.258	100	333	46	86	12	40	5
Dunston, S., Chi.	.260	142	492	59	128	12	50	21
Dykstra, L., Phi.*	.297	63	246	48	73	3	12	24
Elster, K., N.Y.	.241	115	348	33	84	6	36	2
Espy, C., Pit.†	.244	43	82	7	20	1	11	4
Faries, P., S.D.	.177	57	130	13	23	0	7	3
Felder, M., S.F.†	.264	132	348	51	92	0	18	21
Fernandez, T., S.D.†	.272	145	558	81	152	4	38	23
Finley, S., Hou.*	.285	159	596	84	170	8	54	34
Fitzgerald, M., Mon.	.202	71	198	17	40	4	28	4
Fletcher, D., Phi.*	.228	46	136	5	31	1	12	0
Foley, T., Mon.*	.208	86	168	12	35	0	15	2
Galarraga, A., Mon.	.219	107	375	34	82	9	33	5
Gant, R., Atl.	.251	154	561	101	141	32	105	34
Gardner, M., Mon.	.091	27	55	1	5	0	4	0
Gedman, R., St.L.*	.106	46	94	7	10	3	8	0
Gilkey, B., St.L.	.216	81	268	28	58	5	20	14
Girardi, J., Chi.	.191	21	47	3	9	0	6	0
Glavine, T., Atl.*	.230	36	74	1	17	0	6	1
Gonzalez, J., L.A.-Pit.	.042	58	48	5	2	1	3	0
Gonzalez, L., Hou.*	.254	137	473	51	120	13	69	10
Gooden D., N.Y.	.238	27	63	7	15	1	6	1
Grace, M., Chi.*	.273	160	619	87	169	8	58	3
Greene, T., Phi.	.268	38	71	4	19	2	7	0
Gregg, T., Atl.*	.187	72	107	13	20	1	4	2
Griffin, A., L.A.†	.243	109	350	27	85	0	27	5
Grisson, M., Mon.	.267	148	558	73	149	6	39	76
Guerrero, P., St.L.	.272	115	427	41	116	8	70	4
Gwynn, C., L.A.*	.252	94	139	18	35	5	22	1
Gwynn, T., S.D.*	.317	134	530	69	168	4	62	8
Hamilton, J., L.A.	.223	41	94	4	21	1	14	0
Hansen, D., L.A.*	.268	53	56	3	15	1	5	1
Harnisch, P., Hou.	.097	33	62	4	6	0	4	0
Harris, L., L.A.*	.287	145	429	59	123	3	38	12
Hassey, R., Mon.*	.227	52	119	5	27	1	14	1
Hatcher, B., Cin.	.262	138	442	45	116	4	41	11
Hayes, C., Phi.	.230	142	460	34	106	12	53	3

Batter and Team	AVG	G	AB	R	H	HR	RBI	SB
Hayes, V., Phi.*	.225	77	284	43	64	0	21	9
Heath, M., Atl.	.209	49	139	4	29	1	12	0
Herr, T., N.Y.-S.F.†	.209	102	215	23	45	1	21	9
Hill, K., St.L.	.100	30	50	2	5	0	3	0
Hollins, D., Phi.†	.298	56	151	18	45	6	21	1
Howard, T., S.D.†	.249	106	281	30	70	4	22	10
Howell, J., S.D.*	.206	58	160	24	33	6	16	0
Hudler, R., St.L.	.227	101	207	21	47	1	15	12
Hundley, T., N.Y.†	.133	21	60	5	8	1	7	0
Hunter, B., Atl.	.251	97	271	32	68	12	50	0
Hurst, B., S.D.*	.134	31	67	3	9	0	6	0
Jackson, D., S.D.	.262	122	359	51	94	21	49	5
Javier, S., L.A.†	.205	121	176	21	36	1	11	7
Jefferies, G., N.Y.†	.272	136	486	59	132	9	62	26
Johnson, H., N.Y.†	.259	156	564	108	146	38	117	30
Jones, C., Cin.	.292	52	89	14	26	2	6	2
Jordan, R., Phi.	.272	101	301	38	82	9	49	0
Jose, F., St.L.†	.305	154	568	69	173	8	77	20
Justice, D., Atl.*	.275	109	396	67	109	21	87	8
Kennedy, T., S.F.*	.234	69	171	12	40	3	13	0
King, J., Pit.	.239	33	109	16	26	4	18	3
Kingery, M., S.F.*	.182	91	110	13	20	0	8	1
Kruk, J., Phi.*	.294	152	538	84	158	21	92	7
LaValliere, M., Pit.*	.289	108	336	25	97	3	41	2
Lake, S., Phi.	.228	58	158	12	36	1	11	0
Lampkin, T., S.D.*	.190	38	58	4	11	0	3	0
Landrum, C., Chi.*	.233	56	86	28	20	0	6	27
Lankford, R., St.L.*	.251	151	566	83	142	9	69	44
Larkin, B., Cin.	.302	123	464	88	140	20	69	24
Leibrandt, C., Atl.	.043	36	70	1	3	0	2	0
Lemke, M., Atl.†	.234	136	269	36	63	2	23	1
Leonard, M., S.F.*	.240	64	129	14	31	2	14	0
Lewis, D., S.F.	.248	72	222	41	55	1	15	13
Lind, J., Pit.	.265	150	502	53	133	3	54	7
Lindeman, J., Phi.	.337	65	95	13	32	0	12	0
Litton, G., S.F.	.181	59	127	13	23	1	15	0
Lofton, K., Hou.*	.203	20	74	9	15	0	0	2

99

Batter and Team	AVG	G	AB	R	H	HR	RBI	SB
Maddux, G., Chi.	.205	39	88	8	18	1	7	1
Magadan, D., N.Y.*	.258	124	418	58	108	4	51	1
Manwaring, K., S.F.	.225	67	178	16	40	0	19	1
Martinez, C., Pit.-Cin.	.234	64	154	13	36	6	19	0
Martinez, Da., Mon.*	.295	124	396	47	117	7	42	16
Martinez, De., Mon.	.153	32	72	8	11	0	2	0
Martinez, R., L.A.*	.117	33	77	6	9	1	9	0
McClendon, L., Pit.	.288	85	163	24	47	7	24	2
McGee, W., S.F.†	.312	131	497	67	155	4	43	17
McGriff, F., S.D.*	.278	153	528	84	147	31	106	4
McLemore, M., Hou.†	.148	21	61	6	9	0	2	0
McReynolds, K., N.Y.	.259	143	522	65	135	16	74	6
Merced, O., Pit.†	.275	120	411	83	113	10	50	8
Miller, K., N.Y.	.280	98	275	41	77	4	23	14
Mitchell, K., S.F.	.256	113	371	52	95	27	69	2
Mitchell, K., Atl.	.318	48	66	11	21	2	5	3
Morandini, M., Phi.*	.249	98	325	38	81	1	20	13
Morgan, M., L.A.	.092	34	76	2	7	0	3	0
Morris, H., Cin.*	.318	136	478	72	152	14	59	10
Morris, J., Phi.*	.220	85	127	15	28	1	6	2
Mota, A., Hou.	.189	27	90	4	17	1	6	2
Mulholland, T., Phi.	.088	35	80	3	7	0	0	1
Murphy, D., Phi.	.252	153	544	66	137	18	81	1
Murray, E., L.A.†	.260	153	576	69	150	19	96	10
Nabholz, C., Mon.*	.115	24	52	5	6	0	1	0
Nichols, C., Hou.	.196	20	51	3	10	0	1	0
Nixon, O, Atl.†	.297	124	401	81	119	0	26	72
Noboa, J., Mon.	.242	67	95	5	23	1	2	2
O'Brien, C., N.Y.	.185	69	168	16	31	2	14	0
O'Neill, P., Cin.*	.256	152	532	71	136	28	91	12
Oberkfell, K., Hou.*	.229	53	70	7	16	0	14	0
Offerman, J., L.A.†	.195	52	113	10	22	0	3	3
Ojeda, B., L.A.*	.161	31	56	2	9	1	3	0
Olivares, O., St.L.	.226	28	53	4	12	0	6	0
Oliver, J., Cin.	.216	94	269	21	58	11	41	0
Olson, G., Atl.	.241	133	411	46	99	6	44	1
Oquendo, J., St.L.†	.240	127	366	37	88	1	26	1

Batter and Team	AVG	G	AB	R	H	HR	RBI	SB
Ortiz, J., Hou.	.277	47	83	7	23	1	5	0
Owen, S., Mon.†	.255	139	424	39	108	3	26	2
Pagnozzi, T., St.L.	.264	140	459	38	121	2	57	9
Pena, G., St.L.†	.243	104	185	38	45	5	17	15
Pendleton, T., Atl.†	.319	153	586	94	187	22	86	10
Perezchica, T., S.F.	.229	23	48	2	11	0	3	0
Perry, G., St.L.*	.240	109	242	29	58	6	36	15
Portugal, M., Hou.	.196	33	46	4	9	0	3	0
Presley, J., S.D.	.136	20	59	3	8	1	5	0
Quinones, L., Cin.†	.222	97	212	15	47	4	20	1
Ramirez, R., Hou.	.236	101	233	17	55	1	20	3
Rasmussen, D., S.D.*	.136	25	44	3	6	0	0	0
Ready, R., Phi.	.249	76	205	32	51	1	20	2
Redus, G., Pit.	.246	98	252	45	62	7	24	17
Reed, J., Cin.*	.267	91	270	20	72	3	31	0
Reyes, G., Mon.	.217	83	207	11	45	0	13	2
Rhodes, K., Hou.*	.213	44	136	7	29	1	12	2
Rijo, J., Cin.	.209	31	67	7	14	0	5	0
Roberts, L., S.D.†	.281	117	424	66	119	3	32	26
Sabo, C., Cin.	.301	153	582	91	175	26	88	19
Salazar, L., Chi.	.258	103	333	34	86	14	38	0
Samuel, J., L.A.	.271	153	594	74	161	12	58	23
Sandberg, R., Chi.	.291	158	585	104	170	26	100	22
Sanders, D., Atl.*	.191	54	110	16	21	4	13	11
Santiago, B., S.D.	.267	152	580	60	155	17	87	8
Santovenia, N., Mon.	.250	41	96	7	24	2	14	0
Sasser, M., N.Y.*	.272	96	228	18	62	5	35	0
Scioscia, M., L.A.*	.264	119	345	39	91	8	40	4
Scott, G., Chi.	.165	31	79	8	13	1	5	0
Sharperson, M., L.A.	.278	105	216	24	60	2	20	1
Shipley, C., S.D.	.275	37	91	6	25	1	6	0
Simms, M., Hou.	.203	49	123	18	25	3	16	1
Slaught, D., Pit.	.295	77	220	19	65	1	29	1
Smiley, J., Pit.*	.100	33	70	3	7	0	3	0
Smith, B., St.L.	.246	31	65	6	16	0	8	0
Smith, Dw., Chi.*	.228	90	167	16	38	3	21	2
Smith, L., Atl.	.275	122	353	58	97	7	44	9

Batter and Team	AVG	G	AB	R	H	HR	RBI	SB
Smith, O., St.L.†	.285	150	550	96	157	3	50	35
Smith, Z., Pit.*	.183	36	71	3	13	0	10	0
Smoltz, J., Atl.	.108	38	65	7	7	0	3	0
Strawberry, D., L.A.*	.265	139	505	86	134	28	99	10
Templeton, G., S.D.-N.Y.†	.221	112	276	25	61	3	26	3
Teufel, T., N.Y.-S.D.	.217	117	341	41	74	12	44	9
Tewksbury, B., St.L.	.155	30	58	5	9	0	2	0
Thompson, M., St.L.*	.307	115	326	55	100	6	34	16
Thompson, R., S.F.	.262	144	492	74	129	19	48	14
Thon, D., Phi.	.252	146	539	44	136	9	44	11
Tolentino, J., Hou.*	.259	44	54	6	14	1	6	0
Tomlin, R., Pit.*	.192	32	52	5	10	0	2	0
Treadway, J., Atl.*	.320	106	306	41	98	3	32	2
Uribe, J., S.F.†	.221	90	231	23	51	1	12	3
Van Slyke, A., Pit.*	.265	138	491	87	130	17	83	10
Vanderwal, J., Mon.*	.213	21	61	4	13	1	8	0
Varsho, G., Pit.*	.273	99	187	23	51	4	23	9
Villanueva, H., Chi.	.276	71	192	23	53	13	32	0
Viola, F., N.Y.*	.127	35	71	2	9	0	1	0
Vizcaino, J., Chi.†	.262	93	145	7	38	0	10	2
Walker, C., Chi.†	.257	124	374	51	96	6	34	13
Walker, L., Mon.*	.290	137	487	59	141	16	64	14
Wallach, T., Mon.	.225	151	577	60	130	13	73	2
Walton, J., Chi.	.219	123	270	42	59	5	17	7
Ward, K., S.D.	.243	44	107	13	26	2	8	1
Webster, M., Pit.-L.A.†	.222	94	171	21	38	2	19	0
Wehner, J., Pit.	.340	37	106	15	36	0	7	3
Wilkerson, C., Pit.†	.188	85	191	20	36	2	18	2
Wilkins, R., Chi.*	.222	86	203	21	45	6	22	3
Williams, K., Mon.	.271	34	70	11	19	0	1	2
Williams, M., S.F.	.268	157	589	72	158	34	98	5
Wilson, C., St.L.	.171	60	82	5	14	0	13	0
Wilson, T., S.F.*	.235	48	51	7	12	1	5	0
Winningham, H., Cin.*	.225	98	169	17	38	1	4	4
Yelding, E., Hou.	.243	78	276	19	67	1	20	11
Young, G., Hou.†	.218	108	142	26	31	1	11	16
Zeile, T., St.L.	.280	155	565	76	158	11	81	17

NATIONAL LEAGUE
Pitching
(40 or more innings pitched)
*Throws Left-Handed

Pitcher and Team	W	L	ERA	G	IP	H	BB	SO
Agosto, J., St.L.*	5	3	4.81	72	86.0	92	39	34
Akerfelds, D., Phi.	2	1	5.26	30	49.2	49	27	31
Andersen, L., S.D.	3	4	2.30	38	47.0	39	13	40
Armstrong, J., Cin.	7	13	5.48	27	139.2	158	54	93
Ashby, A., Phi.	1	5	6.00	8	42.0	41	19	26
Assenmacher, P., Chi.* ..	7	8	3.24	75	102.2	85	31	117
Avery, S., Atl.*	18	8	3.38	35	210.1	189	65	137
Barnes, B., Mon.*	5	8	4.22	28	160.0	135	84	117
Beck, R., S.F.	1	1	3.78	31	52.1	53	13	38
Belcher, T., L.A.	10	9	2.62	33	209.1	189	75	156
Belinda, S., Pit.	7	5	3.45	60	78.1	50	35	71
Benes, A., S.D.	15	11	3.03	33	223.0	194	59	167
Berenguer, J., Atl.	0	3	2.24	49	64.1	43	20	53
Bielecki, M., Chi.-Atl.	13	11	4.46	41	173.2	171	56	75
Black, B., S.F.*	12	16	3.99	34	214.1	201	71	104
Boever, J., Phi.	3	5	3.84	68	98.1	90	54	89
Bones, R., S.D.	4	6	4.83	11	54.0	57	18	31
Boskie, S., Chi.	4	9	5.23	28	129.0	150	52	62
Bowen, R., Hou.	6	4	5.15	14	71.2	73	36	49
Boyd, D., Mon.	6	8	3.52	19	120.1	115	40	82
Brantley, J., S.F.	5	2	2.45	67	95.1	78	52	81
Browning, T., Cin.*	14	14	4.18	36	230.1	241	56	115
Burke, T., Mon.-N.Y.	6	7	3.36	72	101.2	96	26	59
Burkett, J., S.F.	12	11	4.18	36	206.2	223	60	131
Carpenter, C., St.L.	10	4	4.23	59	66.0	53	20	47

Pitcher and Team	W	L	ERA	G	IP	H	BB	SO
Castillo, F., Chi.	6	7	4.35	18	111.2	107	33	73
Charlton, N., Cin.*	3	5	2.91	39	108.1	92	34	77
Clancy, J., Hou.-Atl.	3	5	3.91	54	89.2	73	34	50
Combs, P., Phi.*	2	6	4.90	14	64.1	64	43	41
Cone, D., N.Y. 14		14	3.29	34	232.2	204	73	241
Cormier, R., St.L.*	4	5	4.12	11	67.2	74	8	38
Corsi, J., Hou.	0	5	3.71	47	77.2	76	23	53
Cox, D., Phi.	4	6	4.57	23	102.1	98	39	46
Crews, T., L.A.	2	3	3.43	60	76.0	75	19	53
Darling, R., N.Y.-Mon. ...	5	8	4.37	20	119.1	121	33	69
DeJesus, J., Phi. 10		9	3.42	31	181.2	147	128	118
DeLeon, J., St.L.	5	9	2.71	28	162.2	144	61	118
Deshaies, J., Hou.*	5	12	4.98	28	161.0	156	72	98
Dibble, R., Cin.	3	5	3.17	67	82.1	67	25	124
Downs, K., S.F. 10		4	4.19	45	111.2	99	53	62
Drabek, D., Pit. 15		14	3.07	35	234.2	245	62	142
Fassero, J., Mon.*	2	5	2.44	51	55.1	39	17	42
Fernandez, S., N.Y.*	1	3	2.86	8	44.0	36	9	31
Franco, J., N.Y.*	5	9	2.93	52	55.1	61	18	45
Fraser, W., St.L.	3	3	4.93	35	49.1	44	21	25
Freeman, M., Atl.	1	0	3.00	34	48.0	37	13	34
Gardner, M., Mon.	9	11	3.85	27	168.1	139	75	107
Glavine, T., Atl.* 20		11	2.55	34	246.2	201	69	192
Gooden, D., N.Y. 13		7	3.60	27	190.0	185	56	150
Gott, J., L.A.	4	3	2.96	55	76.0	63	32	73
Greene, T., Phi. 13		7	3.38	36	207.2	177	66	154
Grimsley, J., Phi.	1	7	4.87	12	61.0	54	41	42
Gross, K., L.A. 10		11	3.58	46	115.2	123	50	95
Gross, K., Cin.	6	4	3.47	29	85.2	93	40	40
Hammond, C., Cin.*	7	7	4.06	20	99.2	92	48	50
Haney, C., Mon.*	3	7	4.04	16	84.2	94	43	51
Harnisch, P., Hou. 12		9	2.70	33	216.2	169	83	172
Harris, G., S.D.	9	5	2.23	20	133.0	116	27	95
Hartley, M., L.A.-Phi.	4	1	4.21	58	83.1	74	47	63
Heaton, N., Pit.*	3	3	4.33	42	68.2	72	21	34
Henry, D., Hou.	3	2	3.19	52	67.2	51	39	51
Hernandez, X., Hou.	2	7	4.71	32	63.0	66	32	55

Pitcher and Team	W	L	ERA	G	IP	H	BB	SO
Hershiser, O., L.A.	7	2	3.46	21	112.0	112	32	73
Hickerson, B., S.F.*	2	2	3.60	17	50.0	53	17	43
Hill, K., St.L. 11		10	3.57	30	181.1	147	67	121
Howell, J., L.A.	6	5	3.18	44	51.0	39	11	40
Hurst, B., S.D.* 15		8	3.29	31	221.2	201	59	141
Innis, J., N.Y.	0	2	2.66	69	84.2	66	23	47
Jackson D., Chi.*	1	5	6.75	17	70.2	89	48	31
Jones, B., Mon.	4	9	3.35	77	88.2	76	33	46
Jones, J., Hou.	6	8	4.39	26	135.1	143	51	88
Kile, D., Hou.	7	11	3.69	37	153.2	144	84	100
Kipper, B., Pit.*	2	2	4.65	52	60.0	66	22	38
LaCross, M., S.F.	1	5	7.23	18	47.1	61	24	30
Lancaster, L., Chi.	9	7	3.52	64	156.0	150	49	102
Landrum, B., Pit.	4	4	3.18	61	76.1	76	19	45
Lefferts, C., S.D.*	1	6	3.91	54	69.0	74	14	48
Leibrandt, C., Atl.* 15		13	3.49	36	229.2	212	56	128
Maddux, G., Chi. 15		11	3.35	37	263.0	232	66	198
Maddux, M., S.D.	7	2	2.46	64	98.2	78	27	57
Mahler, R., Mon.-Atl.	2	4	4.50	23	66.0	70	28	27
Martinez, De., Mon. 14		11	2.39	31	222.0	187	62	123
Martinez, R., L.A. 17		13	3.27	33	220.1	190	69	150
McClellan, P., S.F.	3	6	4.56	13	71.0	68	25	44
McDowell, R., Phi.-L.A.	9	9	2.93	71	101.1	100	48	50
McElroy, C., Chi.*	6	2	1.95	71	101.1	73	57	92
Melendez, J., S.D.	8	5	3.27	31	93.2	77	24	60
Mercker, K., Atl.*	5	3	2.58	50	73.1	56	35	62
Morgan, M., L.A. 14		10	2.78	34	236.1	197	61	140
Mulholland, T., Phi.* 16		13	3.61	34	232.0	231	49	142
Myers, R., Cin.*	6	13	3.55	58	132.0	116	80	108
Nabholz, C., Mon.*	8	7	3.63	24	153.2	134	57	99
Ojeda, B., L.A.* 12		9	3.18	31	189.1	181	70	120
Olivares, O., St.L. 11		7	3.71	28	167.1	148	61	91
Oliveras, F., S.F.	6	6	3.86	55	79.1	69	22	48
Osuna, A., Hou.*	7	6	3.42	71	81.2	59	46	68
Palacios, V., Pit.	6	3	3.75	36	81.2	69	38	64
Patterson, B., Pit.*	4	3	4.11	54	65.2	67	15	57
Pena, A., N.Y.-Atl.	8	1	2.40	59	82.1	74	22	62

Pitcher and Team	W	L	ERA	G	IP	H	BB	SO
Peterson, A., S.D.	3	4	4.45	13	54.2	50	28	37
Portugal, M., Hou.	10	12	4.49	32	168.1	163	59	120
Power, T., Cin.	5	3	3.62	68	87.0	87	31	51
Rasmussen, D., S.D.* ...	6	13	3.74	24	146.2	155	49	75
Righetti, D., S.F.*	2	7	3.39	61	71.2	64	28	51
Rijo, J., Cin.	15	6	2.51	30	204.1	165	55	172
Ritchie, W., Phi.*	1	2	2.50	39	50.1	44	17	26
Robinson, D., ...	5	9	4.38	34	121.1	123	50	78
Rodriquez, R., S.D.*	3	1	3.26	64	80.0	66	44	40
Rojas, M., Mon.	3	3	3.75	37	48.0	42	13	37
Ruffin, B., Phi.*	4	7	3.78	31	119.0	125	38	85
Ruskin, S., Mon.*	4	4	4.24	64	63.2	57	30	46
Sampen, B., Mon.	9	5	4.00	43	92.1	96	46	52
Scanlan, B., Chi.	7	8	3.89	40	111.0	114	40	44
Schilling, C., Hou.	3	5	3.81	56	75.2	79	39	71
Schourek, P., N.Y.*	5	4	4.27	35	86.1	82	43	67
Scudder, S., Cin.	6	9	4.35	27	101.1	91	56	51
Simons, D., N.Y.*	2	3	5.19	42	60.2	55	19	38
Slocumb, H., Chi.	2	1	3.45	52	62.2	53	30	34
Smiley, J., Pit.*	20	8	3.08	33	207.2	194	44	129
Smith, B., St.L.	12	9	3.85	31	198.2	188	45	94
Smith, L., St.L.	6	3	2.34	67	73.0	70	13	67
Smith, P., Atl.	1	3	5.06	14	48.0	48	22	29
Smith, Z., Pit.*	16	10	3.20	35	228.0	234	29	120
Smoltz, J., Atl.	14	13	3.80	36	229.2	206	77	148
Stanton, M., Atl.*	5	5	2.88	74	78.0	62	21	54
Sutcliffe, R., Chi.	6	5	4.10	19	96.2	96	45	52
Terry, S., St.L.	4	4	2.80	65	80.1	76	32	52
Tewksbury, B., St.L.	11	12	3.25	30	191.0	206	38	75
Tomlin, R., Pit.*	8	7	2.98	31	175.0	170	54	104
Viola, F., N.Y.*	13	15	3.97	35	231.1	259	54	132
Walk, B., Pit.	9	2	3.60	25	115.0	104	35	67
Whitehurst, W., N.Y.	7	12	4.19	36	133.1	142	25	87
Whitson, E., S.D.	4	6	5.03	13	78.2	93	17	40
Williams, M., Phi.*	12	5	2.34	69	88.1	56	62	84
Wilson, T., S.F.*	13	11	3.56	44	202.0	173	77	139
Young, A., N.Y.	2	5	3.10	10	49.1	48	12	20

BRUCE WEBER PICKS
HOW THEY'LL FINISH IN 1992

American League East

1. Boston
2. Detroit
3. Toronto
4. Baltimore
5. Milwaukee
6. New York
7. Cleveland

American League West

1. Chicago
2. Texas
3. Oakland
4. California
5. Minnesota
6. Kansas City
7. Seattle

National League East

1. New York
2. Chicago
3. Pittsburgh
4. St. Louis
5. Philadelphia
6. Montreal

National League West

1. Cincinnati
2. Atlanta
3. Los Angeles
4. San Diego
5. San Francisco
6. Houston

American League Champions: Boston
National League Champions: Cincinnati
World Champions: Cincinnati

YOU PICK
HOW THEY'LL FINISH IN 1992

**American League
East**

1.

2.

3.

4.

5.

6.

7.

**American League
West**

1.

2.

3.

4.

5.

6.

7.

**National League
East**

1.

2.

3.

4.

5.

6.

**National League
West**

1.

2.

3.

4.

5.

6.

American League Champions:

National League Champions:

World Champions: